Look what people are saying about Rhonda Nelson...

About *The Ex-Girlfriends' Club*
"Uses well-developed characters in an emotional setting for a stellar story of love reunited."
—*Romantic Times BOOKreviews*

About the Men Out of Uniform miniseries
"*The Player* (4.5) by Rhonda Nelson is a hot, sexy story with great humor and a set-up of wonderful, strong men who it will be a joy to follow in the Men Out of Uniform series."
—*Romantic Times BOOKreviews*

"Ms. Nelson has started an amazing trilogy with the three Rangers. Humor, passion, and a little adventure set the scene for this romance, as these wonderful and somewhat damaged characters come together. Witty dialogue, along with some very touching moments, gives the feeling of realness, while these characters seek to find what they are searching for. I am already excited to see what happens to the next Ranger."
—*Coffee Time Romance*

"As in the first book, the secondary characters fill out the story nicely, and there are I believe two more Chicks who need to get their men even if they don't know it yet. With exciting believable characters and hot passion Rhonda Nelson has created an exciting series, and I can't wait to see who will be getting it next."
—*A Romance Review*

Blaze™

Dear Reader,

Every once in a while I'll fall so in love with a character in one of my books that they more than breathe in my imagination—they breathe on the page. Commitment-phobic bounty hunter Linc Stone is that kind of character. He's tough, rough, gruff, sexy-as-hell, occasionally politically incorrect, wicked, honorable, honest to a fault, adorably clueless at times and completely flawed and lovable. Can you tell I like him? Only the right kind of woman would work for him—the kind who wouldn't take any crap, of course—so pairing him with an über-organized wedding planner who firmly believes in happily ever after was a blast. These characters have been a joy and their story a sheer pleasure to write.

I love to hear from my readers, so be sure to pop by my Web site—www.ReadRhondaNelson.com. I blog daily about the bizarre happenings that make up my everyday life. Sample headings include "Whine About It Wednesday" and "Dear Muse, Could You Please Show Up?"

Happy reading!

Rhonda

FEELING THE HEAT

Rhonda Nelson

HARLEQUIN®

TORONTO • NEW YORK • LONDON
AMSTERDAM • PARIS • SYDNEY • HAMBURG
STOCKHOLM • ATHENS • TOKYO • MILAN • MADRID
PRAGUE • WARSAW • BUDAPEST • AUCKLAND

ISBN-13: 978-0-373-79365-5
ISBN-10:   0-373-79365-0

FEELING THE HEAT

ABOUT THE AUTHOR

A Waldenbooks bestselling author, two-time RITA® Award nominee and *Romantic Times BOOKreviews* Reviewers Choice nominee, Rhonda Nelson writes hot romantic comedy for Harlequin Blaze. In addition to a writing career she has a husband, two adorable kids, a black Lab and a beautiful bichon frise who dogs her every step. She and her family make their chaotic but happy home in a small town in northern Alabama.

Books by Rhonda Nelson

Don't miss any of our special offers. Write to us at the following address for information on our newest releases.

Harlequin Reader Service
U.S.: 3010 Walden Ave., P.O. Box 1325, Buffalo, NY 14269
Canadian: P.O. Box 609, Fort Erie, Ont. L2A 5X3

To Jennifer LaBrecque, my bounty hunter
cohort in crime. Plotting these books with you
has been so much fun. I treasure your friendship.

And to the helpful staff at our local
Sonic Drive-thru for always being so cheerful
when I come by for my usual cup of ice.
You guys are wonderful.

Prologue

CHAMPAGNE CHILLING? Check.

Candles ready? Check.

Favorite chocolates on hand? Check.

Casablanca DVD loaded in player? Check.

Was Georgia Hart planning a seduction? To the casual observer it might look that way, but sadly… no. A droll smile rolled around her lips.

Always a wedding planner, but never a bride.

Carter, her last boyfriend, had exited the scene a couple of weeks ago, a typical end to another disappointing doomed-from-the-start relationship.

Despite the fact that he'd been witty, charming and handsome, when it had come time to take the relationship to the next level—one of the sexual variety— Georgia had been unable to bring herself to do it. Why? Who knew? She'd given it a lot of thought since and still couldn't put her finger on what had been the problem, but there'd been something about him that had prevented her from becoming intimate, a little red flag waving in the back of her mind that heralded a mistake-in-the-making. Having always been one to trust her instincts, she'd muttered several unladylike epithets—she'd wanted to want him, wanted her own happily-ever-after, dammit—but had kindly shown him the door.

Naturally, Carter had taken exception to the fact that she hadn't wanted to sleep with him and had left her house in a huff of anger. She winced, remembering, and hurried upstairs to finish getting ready, leaping over two seriously overweight cats and an incontinent one-eyed Chihuahua with the heart of a Great Dane in the process. The cats—Bogey and Bacall—didn't so much as flinch, but Stitch let out a playful little yap and followed her into her room. Smiling, she bent and patted his knobby little head, then pushed her feet into her shoes.

At any rate, she was adding the finishing touches to her solo celebration, the one she ritualistically hosted for herself after each wedding she'd successfully planned.

Her assistant, Karen, called it anal—Georgia preferred to call it tradition.

Today was another I-Do day, one that had been more than a year in the making. Putting that much effort, hard work and planning into someone else's special day certainly called for a little self-pampering when that day was over, right?

And no doubt she'd needed it. Georgia rolled her eyes. Marrying one of Memphis's most eligible bachelors off to the topless dancer he'd fallen in love with—much to the grief and humiliation of his mortified but stoic family—had been no small feat.

She didn't just deserve a pat on the back—she deserved a damned hot-stone massage administered by a half-naked male model whose spotty English included the phrases "You're lovely, Georgia" and "You're a goddess, Georgia" and "I want you now, Georgia."

Smiling, she padded over to her jewelry box for the last item on her checklist—her mother's engagement ring. Despite the headache, worry, angst and overall hassle of her job, the ring—the stone specifically, though it was essentially worthless—was a tangible reminder of why she did what she did, why she'd gone into the business of love.

The ring was more than an heirloom, more than a sentimental piece of jewelry—it was a symbol of a love so pure and perfect it had fueled her dreams and shaped her destiny. It was why she could do what she did, knowing that more than half of the people she helped marry would ultimately end up divorced. It was why even though she hadn't found it with Carter or any of the guys who'd come before him, she knew that *real* love did exist.

Her parents, God rest their souls, had been living proof of that.

It was why she knew if she was patient, at some point, she'd have her own true love, her own hero, her own family. It was why, at the end of the day, she was a no-holds-barred, hands-down, dyed-in-the-wool *romantic*.

She opened the box and let out a little gasp, which was quickly followed by a sickening wave of horror and dread so intense she swayed from the impact.

Dear God in heaven. Her mother's ring was gone.

1

Four days later…

"SHE WAS HERE AGAIN," Marlene Duncan said as Linc Stone strolled into the office of AA Atco Bail Bonds, Inc., a greasy sack of Memphis's best barbecue in one hand and a six-pack of bottled Coca-Cola in the other.

Linc grimaced. Though a few particularly pissed-off ex-girlfriends had been known to track him down at the office, he instinctively knew that Marlene wasn't talking about one of them. He swore under his breath.

She was talking about *her.*

Georgia Hart, the wedding planner from hell who was having a little trouble with the English language—recognizing the word "no," specifically.

"What did you tell her?"

His father, evidently lured by the smell of barbecue, emerged from his office in the back and snagged a bottle of Coke, then popped the top off using the scarred edge of Marlene's desk. "Tell who what?" Martin wanted to know.

At six-foot-six, his father was a mountain of a man with a patience for fools the size of an anthill. He drove American cars, would only drink Coke out of the bottle—because "plastic was for pussies"—preferred Johnny Cash to Elvis, practically sacrilegious in their neck of the woods, and ate his steaks cooked rare. He'd never met a woman he couldn't charm, and at sixty-two, he could still arm wrestle his sons and win.

Galling, but true.

Marlene frowned at her desk, but refrained from saying anything. Despite the fact that she'd installed a bottle opener on the paneled wall next to Martin's office door, he still refused to use it. Just to annoy her, Linc imagined, smiling. Curiously, it was becoming one of his father's favorite pastimes.

"Ask your father. He's the one who eventually talked to her," Marlene told him. She doled out sandwiches and pulled a bag of gourmet chips from the filing cabinet behind her desk, which doubled as their pantry. He caught a glimpse of chocolate-mint cookies and made a mental note to help himself to a sleeve before he took off again. Cade's trail mix was in there, too, but Linc wasn't interested in that. He grimaced. Cade's "healthy" was Linc's "bird food."

Knowing that his father was a sucker for a sad case and female face, Linc inwardly winced with dread and let go a sigh. "What'd she have to say this time, Dad?"

"Same thing she's been telling you," he said gruffly, crowding onto Marlene's side of the desk. He nudged the paper aside, frowning at another political ad gracing the cover. It was that time of year again. "She just wants to tag along while you look for Carter Watkins. I don't see what the big deal is. She seems smart enough, and I know she's not pinup material, but she wouldn't point if a quail flew through the room, Son." He pulled a shrug. "What would it hurt to let her go with you?"

Marlene heaved a disgusted breath and glared exasperatedly at Martin. "You're a pig, you know that?"

Martin smiled, unrepentant. "I've been called worse."

Linc snagged the nearest chair and commandeered a corner of Marlene's desk, as well, moving her beloved picture of Bear Bryant to the side in the process. A die-hard Alabama fan, Marlene was damned hard to live with during college football season. He unwrapped his sandwich and, ignoring the quail comment, pretended to consider what his father had said.

Pretended being the operative word.

There was no way in hell he planned on letting Georgia Hart "tag along" with him.

"Why don't we let Cade take this one and she can tag along with him?" Linc suggested wearily, knowing the outcome.

Martin mopped a bit of mustard slaw from the corner of his mouth and scowled at his son. "Aw, hell, you know better than that."

Sadly, he did know better. In order to keep everything equitable between him and Cade, his father insisted on a strict case divvying system. Cade took one, Linc took the next one, Cade, Linc, Cade, Linc and so on. It didn't matter if Cade got two back-to-back high-dollar skips and Linc got stuck with two that would barely cover his utility bill. Fair was fair, according to the skewed logic of Martin Stone, and this was the feast or famine nature of the bond business. They could not trade files and, in most cases, couldn't help each other.

Or so they'd been told.

Fortunately, he and Cade were of the same mind that Martin's system wasn't fair and had privately agreed to work together on any file with a ten-grand or higher payout and split the difference. What their dad didn't know wouldn't hurt him and it sure as hell had helped them on occasion.

Linc had actually considered asking Cade to take the Carter Watkins case just so he wouldn't have to deal with Georgia Hart anymore, but it smacked too much of cowardice—of being scared of a girl, for chrissakes—so he'd abandoned the idea.

Frankly, he didn't know why she managed to bother him so much. He selected a chip, finding himself reluctant to even think about her.

For whatever reason, Georgia Hart…unsettled him.

And that was worrisome in and of itself, because Linc Stone had never let a woman intimidate him.

Watching his father suffer after his mother had died in a car crash had given Linc all the evidence he needed to determine that marriage and love, specifically, weren't for him. He'd been twelve at the time and convinced that his father was invincible. Hell, his mother, too, for that matter. At an even five-feet tall, Lucy Stone might have been small, but she'd been a force to be reckoned with. Linc smiled, remembering. His father had always likened her to a summer storm—quick to anger and quicker to forgive.

And, God, how he'd loved her.

The days following his mother's death were just a fuzzy memory of gritty-eyed grief, but his burly father draped over her rosewood coffin, sobbing as though his world had come to an end, was a picture that remained firmly etched in Linc's mind.

For months after she'd passed away, Martin merely sat and drank. Bathing became an afterthought and no doubt Martin would have starved to death—he and Gracie included—if Cade hadn't stepped up and become the parent they'd needed. Cade had made sure their clothes were clean, their bellies full, their homework done. Cade answered the phone calls, assuring the rest of the family they were doing fine, when in reality they'd momentarily lost both parents.

Curiously, they had Memphis Power to thank for ultimately getting their dad back.

Three months after their mother had passed away, they'd come home from school to find that the utilities had been turned off. Martin, red-eyed and half-drunk, still weighting down the recliner, hadn't noticed.

For Cade, who'd been growing increasingly weary of his father's self-absorbed indifference, it had been the last damned straw. He'd *exploded,* much like their mother had in the past when she'd had her fill.

"You didn't just lose a wife, you selfish bastard! We lost a mother! Look at you! Look at us! We don't even have electricity and you're so out of it, you haven't even noticed. Are you going to go pay the fucking power bill, Martin, or are we dead to you, too?"

Whether it was the fact that Cade had finally snapped, called him Martin instead of Dad, used foul language or the "Are we dead to you, too?" Linc couldn't say—probably a combination of all four—but their father finally came around. He'd taken care of the utility bill and brought home a bucket of fried chicken—far from a nutritious meal, but it had been a start in the right direction.

Unfortunately, they'd all four learned lessons from that difficult period of time that had shaped who they were, their perceptions about life in general and how to live it. His father had eventually started dating again, but kept things completely superficial. The world as he'd known it had ended when he'd buried his wife. Though Martin eventually learned to cope, Linc knew there was a part of his father that had died along with her.

Cade had stopped calling their father "Dad" and addressed him simply as Martin. He'd been forced to abandon his own grieving in order to care for the rest of them and had appointed himself the guardian of the family, a job he took extremely seriously.

Linc had learned that love could destroy as easily as it could heal and had decided he didn't want any part of it, and Gracie, bless her heart, had learned that the Stone men didn't have a clue how to deal with raising a girl. She'd survived as best she could living in a house overrun with testosterone. The spitting image of Lucy and having inherited their mother's love of flowers, she'd opened a florist shop downtown and was engaged to be married.

Linc sighed, pleasantly full. No doubt she'd be the only Stone out of their clan tying the knot. Cade dated occasionally, but didn't appear the least bit inclined to settle down. His gaze slid to Marlene, who was currently fussing over the mess his father had made on her desk.

Martin displayed some territorial tendencies when it came to their new secretary, but Linc wasn't sure if it would go anywhere and, unless his father was serious about Marlene, he certainly hoped not. In addition to her baked goods and mother-duck tendencies, she was a crackerjack secretary, and she'd been through absolute hell recently.

After thirty years of marriage, her husband had taken off to Vegas with a local showgirl and promptly impregnated her, a blow that had been particularly tough for Marlene, who'd been unable to conceive. She'd retaliated by cleaning his plow in divorce court and taking half of his retirement. If the slimy bastard ever showed his face in Memphis again, he'd have the Stone clan to deal with.

His father, in particular, seemed entirely too taken with the idea of tearing the cheating bastard apart.

As for Linc himself, marriage simply wasn't in the cards. Even the faintest idea of being permanently attached to a woman made his belly clench with dread and his mouth parch with an emotion eerily similar to fear. It wasn't, of course, because Linc wouldn't allow himself to be afraid of anything.

Furthermore, though he didn't think he'd taken the womanizing to Martin's level, Linc nonetheless didn't form any attachments and made sure whomever he was seeing knew the score going in. He liked his women smart and confident and sexy. Smart women were good conversationalists—he'd never had any patience for stupid. Confident women weren't going to be devastated when the inevitable end came. They typically chalked it up to a good time and moved on.

And a sexy woman… Linc grinned and chewed the inside of his cheek. Well, that was self-explanatory.

For whatever reason, an image of Georgia Hart leapt instantly to mind, causing him to shift in his seat. Was she sexy? Pretty even? Like his father had tactlessly pointed out, not in the traditional pinup way.

She had curly dark hair, which she wore in an uncomfortably tight ponytail, and eyes the shade of a Hershey's kiss. A pert nose, rather chubby cheeks and a rosy mouth that was a little overfull, but seemed to fit her face all the same, rounded out her appearance. Each feature wasn't overtly remarkable, but as a whole made her quite compelling. Furthermore, there was just something about her that made him…itch.

She was obviously smart, put-together, confident and all of the other adjectives that went along with what her chosen profession demanded. There was no such thing as a successful *disorganized* wedding planner, and even though he wasn't in the market for a ceremony, her reputation had preceded her. Gracie, in particular, had mentioned she'd like nothing better than a wedding planned by Weddings With Hart, Georgia's company, but given the way things had been going with the business, Linc suspected Georgia was out of their price range.

At any rate, she was a whirlwind of efficiency, the poster child for the type A mentality. Hell, just looking at her had made him tired.

But then he'd looked closer, and that's where the problem had come in.

While Cade had an uncanny knack for intimidation and kicking ass, Linc's strength was his ability to size a person up. Like an FBI profiler, he could read character and spot a liar in the blink of an eye, an asset that had served him well in the bond business, and in life in general.

It had taken him less than a blink to realize that Georgia Hart was the most *organized mess* he'd ever seen.

Perfect presentation and attention to detail aside, she was a wreck. She was a tornado of shame and fear, and if he wasn't careful, he knew he'd get sucked into her storm. Though he didn't know the significance—and frankly didn't want to so that he wouldn't be inclined to help her—losing her mother's ring had hit her hard. It was that fix-me factor of hers that tugged at his shrunken heartstrings and made him feel like his body was getting a little too big for his skin. He didn't know why, but every alarm he had was ringing where she was concerned and he knew his best bet was to stay the hell away from her.

So could she tag along?

Hell no.

Besides, he had too many other things to worry about at the moment—True Blue American Bail Bonds being at the top of his list. The frisky new company had opened up a few doors down on Poplar Street, and had promptly embarked on a heavy ad campaign, which had, unfortunately, cut a sizable chunk out of their profits. Martin and Cade had been discussing the problem one day while Linc was out picking up a skip and had elected him to take care of it. Typical, he thought, smothering a snort. Just exactly what the hell he was supposed to do remained to be seen, but he'd think of something.

Provided he could spend a little less time dodging Georgia Hart and more time in the office.

"You really won't reconsider?" Marlene asked, her expression hopeful on the wedding planner's behalf. A romantic softie, their secretary had immediately been sympathetic to Georgia's plight. "She just wants to do something proactive. You gotta respect that, right?"

Linc wadded his sandwich wrapper into a ball and lobbed it toward the trash can. "It's not about respect, Marlene. It's business. And that's not how we do business." He stood. "Hand me some of those cookies out of the filing cabinet, would you? I've got to go find Carter freakin' Watkins." Linc grimaced.

Preferably before Georgia Hart found *him* again.

2

"GEEZ, GOD, WOMAN. You again?" Linc Stone muttered irritably, passing a hand over his perpetually shadowed jaw.

As Georgia had expected, he wasn't happy to see her on his doorstep, but it could have been avoided if he would have kindly returned her calls.

He didn't, thus she was here. On the threshold of his lair.

Ignoring the wild thump of her pulse, Georgia rolled her eyes and pushed past a disturbingly shirtless and too sexy Linc Stone, bounty hunter extraordinaire and all-around pain in the ass. "Is your phone broken?" she asked.

She scanned his downtown Memphis loft apartment, surprised to discover it wasn't littered with empty pizza boxes and beer bottles, but instead housed a clean combination of beat-up antiques, modern art and eclectic pottery. In fact, Georgia thought, studying a bowl on his coffee table, she suspected she had some pieces from the very same artist. An acoustic guitar which had a well-loved and used air about it stood against the wall and a hint of patchouli hung in the air, the exotic scent seemingly as out of place as she felt. She frowned, unable to make the decor match its obvious occupant.

Perpetually disheveled and irreverent, with dark green eyes that were equally somnolent and sharp, and tousled espresso curls that were in desperate need of a trim, she'd pegged Linc Stone for a Peter Pan eternal frat boy kind of guy, not the hip urban professional who evidently lived here. In fact, the only thing she could say actually matched Linc to the apartment was the location. Just a stone's throw from Beale Street; the moody, bluesy area matched his personality perfectly. Like the infamous area, he was smooth and soulful with a hint of wicked and untold secrets.

Furthermore, Linc fully clothed made her pulse purr—Linc half-naked made it roar. Inconvenient? Insane? Ridiculous?

All of the above, but that didn't change the fact that when she looked at him, she wanted to lick him from head to toe. *Very slowly.*

"No, my phone's not broken," he growled, then shot her a mocking half grin which showcased his perfectly even teeth. "By all means, come on in."

"Thank you," she said, smiling sweetly just to antagonize him. "I think I will."

He shut the door and padded barefoot behind her into the living room. Heaven help her, even his feet were sexy, Georgia thought dimly. "I'm leaving soon, so you'll have to make this quick. What made you think my phone was broken?"

He probably had a dinner date with someone equally gorgeous, Georgia decided, ignoring the little pinprick of misplaced disappointment which landed in her chest. With more bravado that she actually possessed, she settled herself into a comfy armchair near the stacked stone fireplace and stared up at him. To her dismay, another tingle of unwanted heat curled through her middle, forcing her to clear her throat. "You never returned my calls."

Linc bared his teeth in a grin she found strangely thrilling. "That's because I have nothing more to say to you." He shoved his fingers into his loose curls, clearly exasperated. "Why do you keep hounding me?"

Trying to ignore the dark line of hair which bisected his impressive belly and disappeared beneath the waistband of his low-slung jeans, Georgia soldiered on. She was here to get his cooperation and she didn't plan to leave until she had it. If there was a silver lining to him having a date—and that was a big if—it would be that he'd be pressed for time.

"Look, I've simply asked you to let me help you find a certain FTA you're looking for." Carter Failing To Appear in court—thus his status as an FTA— actually worked to her advantage. It meant she wasn't the only person looking for the sonofabitch. "It's not like I've asked you for an arm, for pity's sake."

Feigning bewilderment, Linc scratched his ad- mittedly beautiful head and stared at her. "I dis- tinctly remember telling you that it was out of the question."

"Faulty memory," she quipped, sinking farther into the chair. "There's an herbal supplement for that."

He scowled. "I don't need a damned herbal sup- plement, Ms. Hart. I need you to take no for an answer."

Georgia smiled and shook her head, silently wish- ing it were that simple. "Sorry. It's not going to happen."

Every hint of humor vanished from his face. "Neither is you tagging along with me while I try to find your ex-boyfriend."

Georgia squelched the rising sense of panic in her chest and conjured a smile. "I never said I wanted to 'tag along.' I've offered to help." *You beautiful, thick- headed moron,* she added silently. "There's a differ- ence. Besides, I don't think you understand. I—"

"No, Ms. Hart," he interrupted, his voice a low, frustrated growl. "I think *you're* the one with the communication problem. You made a request. I said no. It's as simple as that." He suddenly grimaced, as though a thought had just struck. "Who gave you my address?"

"Your father. He's a nice man."

"With a death wish," Linc muttered, passing a hand over his face. "Look, when I find Carter Watkins, you'll be the first to know."

"I don't want to be the first to know—I want to be first on the scene." *I want to tackle him to the ground and throttle the whereabouts of my mother's ring from his freakishly small neck. I want to unleash every bit of heartache, anger and frustration his theft has wrought upon my nerves. I want to slug him for duping me and making me feel stupid. I want to rub his face in goose shit and—*

"Ms. Hart?" Linc said questioningly, interrupting her beating-the-crap-out-of-Carter fantasy.

Georgia blinked. "Call me Georgia, please. After all," she insisted doggedly, "we're going to be working together."

He pulled in a deep beleaguered breath as though summoning patience from a higher source. "For the last time, the answer is *no*. I will call you when I find him. I'm looking for him. It's only a matter of time."

A touch of unexpected sympathy softened his gaze. "You know that it's probably gone, right? Finding him doesn't mean you'll find your mother's ring."

So he remembered, Georgia thought, slightly heartened. She'd thought everything she'd said had merely gone in one beautiful ear and out the other. Still...

"I know the odds are against me, yes," she told him. "But that's not going to stop me. I have to find that ring, and I won't quit until I do."

"I don't understand," Linc said, shooting her a measuring look that made the back of her neck burn. "I thought you said the ring was worthless."

"No, I said that it didn't have much monetary value. But it's far from w-worthless." A lump formed in her throat and she silently swore, determined not to cry. In the first place, crying wouldn't put her any closer to her goal, and in the second place, crying in front of Linc Stone was out of the question. It would only solidify her place as a liability.

As a wedding planner, Georgia had the type A tendency down to a science. She was good at organizing, seeing a mess and figuring out the best way to organize the chaos. She could soothe a nervous bride, solve any catering snafu and mend a busted seam at a moment's notice.

In fact, she was so good at what she did she was a bride's best friend and a potential boyfriend's worst nightmare. Had she stepped on a few toes? Certainly. But she'd never hurt anyone. Still, she…intimidated people. She knew that. But she couldn't seem to help herself. She was always looking for the quickest way to streamline any problem—point A to point B in the most efficient manner.

In this case, while she could look for Carter on her own—and no doubt find him—hooking up with someone else who had a vested interest in locating her kleptomaniac ex-boyfriend—namely the bond-enforcement agent who'd posted bail for the thieving bastard—offered the best-case scenario for expediting the matter and resolving the issue at hand.

In short, she needed Linc Stone.

Linc's company had posted bond for Carter after his arrest—the fool had been caught shoplifting a bottle of cologne at a local drugstore. Vain bastard, Georgia thought. Though her knowledge of bounty hunting was pretty vague, Georgia had basic understanding of how it worked. Linc's company posted bond so that Carter could leave jail until his scheduled court date. When Carter missed the court date, the bond was forfeited…which meant Linc's family was stuck holding the bag until they could get Carter's miserable ass back in front of the judge. Personally, after meeting Linc and his father, she wouldn't want to be on their bad side.

Linc inclined his head. "Sentimental value isn't worth jack at a pawn shop, sweetheart, which is more than likely where he's taken it."

"Precisely," Georgia said, straightening her sleeve, a pathetic attempt to regain her composure. "I've already been to every pawn shop in a fifty-mile radius and found his usual haunts. Bill at Sam's Pawn on Hollister distinctly remembers the ring. He offered Carter twenty bucks for it and Carter got pissed off and wouldn't sell it. That was last Thursday," Georgia pointed out.

His gaze sharpened. "The day before he skipped."

"Right. Which means he's still got it. He's holding out for a better offer."

"Why does he think it's worth more?"

Georgia released a heavy sigh. "It's a big stone, but it's hopelessly flawed. It looks impressive until it's put under a loupe."

Linc grimaced. "If that's the case, he'd be better off selling it to some Joe on the street."

Dare she hope they were on the same page? Georgia stood and took a step forward. "Which is exactly why finding him immediately is imperative. If he sells it to some Joe on the street, I'm never going to find it."

"What makes you think he's still in the area?"

She rolled her eyes. "The idiot couldn't even post

bond," she said, disgusted once again at her own stupidity. Why hadn't she heeded her instincts? She'd known—*known*—that something had been off about him. "How the hell is he going to scrape up the money to leave town?"

Linc nodded, seemingly impressed. "His last known address was a motel out by the airport. Was that where he was living when you were seeing him?"

Georgia felt her cheeks burn and looked away. "He was always in a different motel when I was seeing him," she admitted. She cleared her throat, preparing for humiliation. "He told me that he was an adjustor for a national car-insurance chain and this was part of his district, that he was based out of Nashville. His car had the s-sticker," she finished lamely, darting him a look. "I just thought— Look, we only dated for a month. By the time I realized my mother's ring was missing, we'd been over for a couple of weeks." No doubt they would have been over that night whether she'd slept with him or not, Georgia thought, eternally thankful that she'd had sense enough to kick his ass to the curb before that had happened.

Linc considered her with those intense green eyes, inadvertently making another jolt of longing lodge in her belly. "What made you suspect him?"

She could tell the truth, that he was the only man who'd been in her new house and therefore she knew it *had* to be him, but it seemed too pathetic to share. "I read about his arrest in the paper," Georgia improvised, which wasn't a complete lie. She had read about it in the paper. Carter had been dubbed "The Brut Bandit" by the local media. She tucked a stray curl behind her ear, wishing she hadn't taken her hair down before she'd come over here. Between the plump cheeks and cursed curls, she looked like a supersize Shirley Temple. "It didn't take much to put it together."

He nodded, though his skeptical expression told her that he doubted her story. Let him doubt, Georgia thought, lifting her chin. So long as he didn't know the truth, the less foolish she would feel.

And considering that she felt like the biggest moron in the northern hemisphere, she'd take it where she could get it.

Linc shoved a hand through his hair, pushing the dark locks off his forehead. "I still don't understand why this is so important to you," he said. "Why can't you chalk it up to a bad mistake and move on?"

Even if she were wired that way—which she wasn't—letting this go simply wasn't an option. What if her father had had that attitude? Georgia thought. No. It just wasn't even a possibility. The ring, and what it stood for to her and her family's history, was simply too important.

She strolled over to his fireplace and inspected a few photos on the antique Victorian mantel. A picture of what must have been his mother and father stood in the middle, flanked by various snapshots of Linc, his brother, Cade, and his sister, Gracie. Having worked on the same weddings from time to time, Georgia had actually met Linc's little sister. She was a very talented florist—one of the best in the area in Georgia's opinion—fun, a bit in-your-face, but she'd liked her all the same. Linc and Cade shared their father's good looks—the same bold brow, large build and strong jaw. Gracie was the petite image of their mother, a blue-eyed blonde with the same mischievous twinkle in her eye. A beautiful family, she thought.

She had a brother and some distant cousins around town, but other than that, she was on her own. She and Jack shared the family property, but Jack, being the oldest and at the helm of Hart Diversified Industries, had moved into their parents' house on their farm in Germantown after they'd passed away. Sadly, they'd both drowned while on vacation in the Bahamas. Her mother had been caught in a riptide and her father, ever the gallant hero, had gone in to save her. Neither one of them had survived.

Better they'd died together than apart, though, Georgia always thought. They would have been miserable had it been any other way.

Having always been close to Jack, but in need of her own place—particularly because living together wasn't conducive to either one of their love lives, though admittedly Jack's was more active than hers—Georgia had ultimately built on the family property. A strong sentimental streak and a love of old houses had propelled her to build a replica of the Sears Roebuck kit house her grandparents had built in the early nineteen-twenties. Back then the entire house was shipped via railcar and everything was included, right down to the several hundred pounds of nails it would take to put it together.

The house was called The Chelsea, a two-story beauty with a big front porch and large airy rooms. Originally the house had only one bathroom, so Georgia had amended the plan to accommodate a more modern lifestyle. At some point—and her maternal clock was definitely ticking a little louder of late—she wanted to raise a family there.

But first things first, Georgia thought, pulling in a bracing breath. "Have you ever heard of Crater of Diamonds State Park?"

Linc nodded. "It sounds familiar."

"It's over in Arkansas. It's a keep-what-you-find

mining park. My father's parents were farmers, Mr. Stone. My mother's father was a successful banker," she said wryly. "To say that they weren't happy that their daughter had fallen in love with a 'dirt-poor farm boy' would be a mild understatement. When my father went to my grandfather and asked for my mother's hand in marriage, my grandfather laughed at him and said, 'I tell you what, boy. When you can put a two-carat stone on my daughter's hand, I'll give you my blessing.'"

Linc's eyes lit with intrigue and he nodded, encouraging her to go on.

A fond smile turned Georgia's lips as she remembered. "Well, you can imagine how my dad felt. He was working at a local factory—one he would eventually own, by the way," she added proudly. "But a two-carat stone was out of the question. He knew that he couldn't afford it. But my dad…" Georgia sighed. "Dad was resourceful and, more importantly, he loved my mother. So every weekend for a year and a half he went over to the park and he dug and sifted and screened through dirt until he found a two-carat stone." Georgia pulled a shrug. "Was it worth anything? Nah," she said, shaking her head. "Like I said, it was flawed. But it didn't matter. Grandpa hadn't said the stone had to be perfect, he'd merely indicated the size. And ultimately, he was a man of his word."

Linc leaned a shoulder against the wall. "That's quite a story."

Georgia looked out window, gazed unseeingly at the various lights illuminating the darkness and let go a small breath. "They were quite a pair," she said quietly. "Years later, Dad gave Mom a ring that was twice as big and perfect, but she rarely wore it. She said her original engagement ring might not have the first four C's—cut, clarity, color and carat—but it had one that was far more important. It had character." She felt her eyes mist once again and muttered a hot curse. "And I lost it."

The silence yawned between them and for a moment she didn't think he was going to respond. "Every weekend for a year and half, eh?" he finally asked.

She chuckled, releasing the sob stuck in her throat. "Dad was stubborn."

"So I guess you come by it honestly then."

She managed a weak smile. "I guess I do." She paused and chewed her bottom lip. "Look, I know this isn't your usual style, and I understand that." And she really did. She was asking for admittance onto his turf. It would be like him coming into her office and asking to consult on a wedding. She got that. But... "But I need to do this. I can't *not* do it. Does that make sense?"

Seemingly thawing, Linc looked away and swore under his breath.

He was weakening, Georgia thought, a burst of hope rushing through her. "I can either go with you and help, or follow you around and be a pain in the ass."

He turned to glare at her, but softened it with a hint of a smile that bordered close enough to wicked to make her belly tremble and her nipples pearl. "Either way you're a pain in the ass."

Time to move in for the kill. "Your father tells me that your little sister is getting married next year, tentatively planned for the fall?"

"Yes," he said guardedly, clearly suspecting a trap. "She is."

And his father—a helpfully chatty fellow, who'd clearly had his own agenda when he'd talked to her this morning when she'd gone by the bond office in another futile attempt to talk to Linc—had also told her that they'd lost their mother twenty years ago, and dealing with all the froufrou, girly things a wedding entailed was going to be a "freakin' nightmare." As the only girl and a haunting replica of her mother, Gracie was the apple of the Stone clan's eye. They loved her to distraction. They wanted to make her happy.

Linc, in particular, according to Martin, wanted to make her happy. Evidently the two shared a uniquely special bond.

As the premiere wedding planner in the area, this worked in Georgia's favor, so she pressed her advantage.

"If you help me—if you let me come along with you—I'll plan her wedding." She steepled her fingers beneath her chin and delivered the coup de grâce. *"Gratis."*

Another hot oath slipped from between his sinfully carnal lips, blistering the air and warming her heart.

His gaze tangled with hers, momentarily snatching the breath from her lungs. "Did my father put you up to this?"

"He might have planted the idea," she conceded, instinctively knowing that he would be able to tell if she lied. Judging from the keen look in those sharp green eyes, she got the feeling Linc Stone didn't miss much, if anything.

He swore again and looked away, defeated but not ready to fold.

I've got him, Georgia thought, smiling.

Mission accomplished.

"Fine," he finally said. "But we do this my way and you follow my rules to the letter."

Provided his rules made sense, she'd do just that. If they didn't, well…

She'd improvise.

3

"SO YOU CAVED?"

Sitting in the kitchen of Cade's old farmhouse—the one that belonged to their maternal grandparents—watching his brother cook their steaks over the Jenn-Air grill, Linc resisted the immediate impulse to thump Cade on the back of the head. Satisfying though it may be, they'd gotten a little too old to wrestle. Not that they hadn't done their share of it in the past, he thought, feeling his lips twitch. And he had the scars to prove it. But he liked to think they'd both matured, at least a little bit.

"No, I didn't cave," Linc said, careful to keep the annoyance out of his voice because Cade would pounce on it. He casually tipped his beer back and swallowed. "I merely decided that her offer was too good to refuse." Not a complete lie, if not the complete truth.

Seemingly unconvinced, Cade snorted under his breath. "Admit it. She played you."

"If anyone played me, it was Dad," Linc told him with a significant grimace. "He's the one who told Georgia about Gracie's wedding. What was I supposed to say when she offered to plan it for free? No?" He grunted. "I didn't have a choice."

Cade merely arched a brow.

Ordinarily Linc didn't like being manipulated, but in this instance Martin's interference had allowed him to save a little face because after hearing why the ring was so important to Georgia, Linc wouldn't have been able to turn her away. Hell, she was a pain in the ass, but he wasn't an ogre.

If nothing else, he had to respect the lengths to which Georgia's father had gone to make her mother his bride. Did he understand it? No, of course not, and frankly, he didn't want to. The idea of being that in love with someone—that dependent on another person for his own joy—didn't appeal to him in the least.

If that was love, then he'd leave it to them.

But the idea of the ring being with a thieving bastard like Carter Watkins was simply more than he could take. It grated on every righteous and just nerve in his body, and he liked to think there were a lot of them.

Being in the bond business was ugly work—they typically dealt with the dregs of society, but there was something about a damned thief that just made his blood boil. It was a lazy, disrespectful crime designed to profit off another person's work, and it pissed him off to no end.

Furthermore, it hit too close to home.

Shortly after moving into his loft, he'd been the victim of a break-in. In addition to taking everything of value—mostly electronics and a couple of guns, one of which had belonged to his grandfather—the bastards had trashed everything that wasn't deemed "marketable." Pictures had been taken off the walls and tossed, cushions slashed, his pottery—some of his earlier work that he'd been particularly proud of—had been smashed just for the hell of it. Drawers had been emptied out, tables upended. He'd walked in on a nightmare and to this day, still got that same sick, violated feeling in the pit of his belly when he thought about it.

Just knowing that strangers had entered his own private space—his castle, the one he'd painstakingly worked and saved for—had been enough to make him alternately want to vomit and smash things. Unfortunately, and to his eternal irritation, the perps had never been caught and not a single stolen item had been found. Another reason he suspected that Georgia's ring would forever be MIA. Though it sucked, Carter Watkins could have done anything with it by now. Another flash of anger tightened his jaw.

Finding the man was his job, Linc knew, but knowing firsthand the hurt and hell Carter had put Georgia through over the past few days irritated and annoyed him beyond what was rational. Another alarm bell sounded, alerting him to possible trouble, but like the others, he decided to ignore it. Though Linc had several files open at the moment, Carter Watkins' case had just been moved to the top of his stack. And if he happened to beat the hell out of him in the process of bringing him in, well…so be it.

Georgia had been right on several points, a fact that he had to admit he found impressive. The slime-ball hadn't been able to make bond, which meant funds were low. If funds were low, leaving the area didn't seem plausible. And if he couldn't get a decent price out of the ring at a pawn shop, then duping someone on the street seemed like the next logical course of action. Linc took another pull from his beer. And like she'd already concluded, if Watkins managed to do that, finding the ring would become next to impossible.

"You would have done the same thing," Linc told him, referencing his arrangement with Georgia once more.

Cade paused and shot him a look. "No, I wouldn't."

"Bullshit. For Gracie?" he scoffed. "You know damn well you would've taken the deal, as well."

His brother plated the steaks, added his signature sautéed mushrooms, then made his way over to the big beat-up table that had seen its fair share of Stone gatherings. "No, I wouldn't, because there would have never been a 'deal.' I would have let her come along with me from the start." He seated himself and that too-shrewd gaze caught Linc's. "What interests me is the fact that you said no to start with, little brother. It begs a lot of intriguing questions, if you ask me."

Linc carved a piece of steak off and impaled it on his fork, resisting the urge to shift uncomfortably. "Nobody's asking you."

Infuriatingly, Cade merely smiled. "Have you told Gracie yet?"

Linc nodded, thankful for the shift in conversation. "Yeah. I called her from my cell on the way out here." He chuckled, secretly pleased that he'd made her happy. "She was over the moon. Kept whooping and hollering in my ear."

Interestingly, while discerning the Stone men's thoughts was a bit like trying to decipher ancient Greek, no one ever had to wonder about what Gracie Stone thought or felt. She was an open book, and a loud one at that. Of course, if she'd been quiet when they were growing up, she would have never been heard. While their entire family was admittedly close, there'd been a special bond borne between the two of them after their mother had died. Cade had stepped in and became more of a parent than their father, but he and Gracie had actually been able to remain true siblings. Thankfully she'd found someone who appreciated her exuberant personality and didn't try to tone her down.

Mark Fletcher had been Gracie's high-school sweetheart. He was the strong, silent type. The calm to her storm. Linc grinned. And the guy had balls, too, because dating Gracie knowing that her brothers were waiting in the wings to rip him limb from limb if he hurt their little sister was a testament to stones if there ever was one.

"She told me to tell you that she was sorry she couldn't make it," Linc told him. "She's got a funeral tomorrow and two weddings this weekend." He ate a mushroom and grunted with caveman appreciation. "What was Dad's excuse?"

They generally got together for dinner at Cade's at least two or three times a week. While Martin might be the genetic head of the family, Cade was their unspoken leader and had been ever since their mother died. Holidays, family gatherings…all took place at his brother's house.

Cade grimaced. "Why else? He had a date."

Linc nodded, unsurprised. Their father kept a

sizable pool of eligible women in his dating queue at all times, and seemed to be going out with more frequency and fervor since Marlene had come to work for them. Though it could only be a coincidence, Linc didn't think so. Cade had noticed the recent development, as well, and, like him, suspected Martin was trying too hard to stay busy. But better that than trying too hard with Marlene. Both he and Cade had made it abundantly clear that messing around with their secretary would *not* be cool.

Father or no, they had to draw the line somewhere.

"This is good," Linc said, gesturing toward his steak with his loaded fork.

"Thanks," Cade murmured. He washed a bite down with a bit of wine, or hoity-toity juice as Linc liked to call it. "So what's next for you and Ms. Hart?"

Back to that again, were they? "I'm picking her up at her office in the morning."

"Where's her office?"

"Germantown. We're going to check out a few places we know Watkins has stayed in the past."

"She dated him, right? Doesn't she have a phone number for him? Has she tried getting in touch with him since she discovered the ring missing?"

Marlene certainly hadn't wasted any time bringing Cade up to speed, Linc thought, studying his brother. "She'd been calling a disposable cell. I figure he chucked it after he took the ring." And though she hadn't said it, Linc figured Watkins had chucked her, as well. Talk about adding insult to injury. Take the most important thing in the world away from her, then dump her? Yeah, that's classy. He wiped his mouth and tossed the napkin onto his plate. How the hell had she ended up with loser like him in the first place? Linc wondered, annoyed beyond reason. It boggled the mind.

"Slick bastard, isn't he?"

"He won't be slick enough," Linc said, a bit of a growl creeping into his voice.

Cade paused and studied him. "You sound determined."

Linc chuckled darkly. "You should hear her."

Honestly, Carter Watkins wasn't safe until she found that ring, and he wasn't certain the guy would be even then. Making an enemy of Georgia Hart was probably the stupidest thing the guy had ever done, and considering he wasn't particularly smart, that was saying something.

"She's already proved that she's determined. She didn't give up on you, did she?"

Linc felt a grin catch the corner of his mouth. He had to admit having her show up at his place tonight had been completely unexpected. In fact, when he'd opened the door, it had taken him a couple of seconds to even recognize her.

Her hair had thrown him. It had been down, curling gently around her face and over her shoulders, instead of pulled tight in that infernal ponytail. Honestly, the ponytail wasn't flattering. You'd think she'd have a friend or someone to tell her that she looked better with her hair down. It…softened her, for lack of a better explanation. And considering that he was already susceptible to that vulnerable fix-me thing she had going on, Linc didn't need her to look any softer.

Furthermore—disturbingly—it was damned sexy.

While the too-tight ponytail screamed "Do not touch," the loose spirals coiling around her face practically begged to be wrapped around his fingers. The unrestrained, uninhibited curls, combined with that overly ripe mouth he couldn't seem to stop looking at and wanting to taste, and those sweet melting chocolate eyes, made her infinitely more appealing that he'd originally thought. Had he missed something to begin with? Linc wondered, shifting in his chair as the blood rushed to his loins. Or had he simply not looked close enough?

In the end, it didn't matter.

He was supposed to be looking for Carter Watkins, not looking at her mouth, mooning over her curls and admiring her moxie, dammit.

He'd do good to remember that, a reminder he grimly suspected would become rote over the next few days.

"Now will you tell me why you made me rent *Dog, The Bounty Hunter: Season Three?*" Karen, her assistant, asked with humorous disdain as she breezed into Georgia's living room bearing the DVD and Chinese take-out. Stitch barked madly and ran in circles around her feet while Bogey and Bacall merely looked on in haughty feline arrogance.

Georgia shifted the how-to books she'd purchased on her way home from Linc's apartment to the side of the coffee table, making room for their food. *A Girl's Guide to Bounty Hunting,* the most useful manual so far, sat on top of the stack. Yes, her window of opportunity to prepare herself for their first round of bounty hunting in the morning was rapidly closing, but that didn't mean that she wasn't going to try and cram as much knowledge of the subject as she possibly could into her brain before then. She'd pulled many an all-nighter in college during exams, so she was familiar with the process. And if it helped her keep her mind off of Linc and his probable date—the one she kept telling herself she shouldn't care about—then all the better.

"All in good time," Georgia told her. "All in good

time. What do you want to drink? I've got sweet tea, sweet tea or sweet tea."

Karen carefully set the food on the table and dropped her newest designer bag—an addiction more than a fashion statement—onto the nearest chair. "I think I'll have tea," she replied drolly.

"Excellent choice," Georgia said, making her way into the kitchen.

"I noticed Jack's car was home," she said, obviously fishing for information. "No date tonight?"

Georgia felt a smile tug at her lips. "I guess not. He and Monica exited into Splitsville last weekend."

Knowing the huge crush Karen was nursing on her brother, Georgia really should have mentioned Jack's new unattached status earlier, but she didn't want Karen to get her hopes up. Though it pained her to say it…Karen wasn't exactly Jack's type. Which was too bad because if she could handpick a sister-in-law, Karen would fit the bill perfectly. She was smart, ambitious and loyal. She was also a little bit…forthright. An excellent quality for an assistant, but could be quite daunting and abrasive to a potential mate. Beneath the bravado though, Karen was a good-hearted softie who desperately wanted her happily-ever-after.

With Jack, specifically, if Georgia's instincts were on target.

She'd casually put out a couple of feelers to her brother regarding any romantic interest in Karen, and his reaction had been short and to the point.

Hell, no.

Personally, given the amiable yes-girls her brother typically dated, Georgia thought a dose of unaccommodating directness was exactly what Jack needed. She wouldn't interfere though, because she sure as hell wouldn't want Jack interfering in her love life. And, considering how protective of her he was, she knew that was a too-real possibility. In fact, she typically kept her dates away from her brother.

"A Girl's Guide to Bounty Hunting? Skip Tracing 101? Bond Enforcement Procedure for Dummies?" Karen called out from the living room, her voice escalating and more bewildered with each title. "Are, uh… Are you thinking about making a career change? Because if you are, as your assistant, this would fall firmly into the need-to-know category."

Dumping ice into glasses, Georgia chuckled softly and shook her head. "No."

Thumbing through one of the books, Karen appeared in the kitchen doorway. She quirked a brow. "Then why all the how-to books? Why the bounty hunter DVD?" She frowned ominously. "Have you developed a fetish I don't know about?"

Georgia pulled a couple of plates from the

cabinet, snagged forks, then gestured for Karen to bring the tea. She headed back to the living room. "Of course not," she said, rolling her eyes. Honestly, sometimes Karen's imagination was quite…odd.

"Then what's going on?"

Part of the reason she'd hired Karen was for her persistence, but she wasn't accustomed to having that dog-with-a-bone tenacity directed at her. Nevertheless, she'd enlisted Karen's help and would be depending heavily upon her to hold down the fort during her absence over the next few days. At least, she hoped it was only a few days. Anything beyond that spelled defeat, a possibility she refused to even entertain.

Georgia released a pent-up breath. "I'm going to be working with a bounty hunter over the next few days and I want to have a general idea of what to expect."

Karen dropped onto the couch and stared at her in apparent disbelief. "A bounty hunter?"

Georgia nodded. The inevitable why would come shortly, so she took advantage of Karen's momentary shock to load her plate with a helping of fried rice and sweet-and-sour chicken. Where was her egg roll? she wondered, pilfering through the take-out bag. She knew she'd ordered one. Dammit, if they'd forgotten her egg roll—

"Okay, you got me. Why are you going to be working with a b-bounty hunter?"

"He's looking for Carter Watkins and it's in my best interest to find him, as well." That was the vague answer. She knew she'd have to pony up the complete truth, but even telling Karen—who admittedly was a good friend, if not her best friend—was absolutely mortifying. Her cheeks burned just thinking about it. Karen wouldn't judge, she knew, and would be an instant ally, but even knowing that didn't keep her from feeling *enormously* stupid.

How in the hell could she have been such a poor judge of character? How could she have been so easily fooled? Had she been that desperate for a little romance—for what her parents had shared—that she'd overlooked obvious flaws? God help her, had she been that needy? She'd like to think that wasn't the case, but she'd allowed a man into her home who'd stolen her most prized possession. She made a moue of self-disgust. Clearly she'd made a grievous mistake somewhere along the way.

But no more.

She would no longer be actively looking for love. After this final disastrous outcome, love would simply have to find her.

Granted, being of the proactive nature, this would be a big change for her. For as long as she could remember, Georgia had been a goal-setter. Eyes on the prize and all that. In grade school it had been honor roll. In college, the dean's list. In business, nothing short of getting her masters from Wharton would do. She'd built the most successful business of its kind in the area and was proud of her accomplishments.

Though she'd inherited a modest fortune from her parents and grandparents, she'd wanted to make her own way. As such, other than the property on which her house stood, every penny that had gone into building her dream home had been made via the sweat of *her* brow, not someone else's. For whatever reason, that had been incredibly important to her. Furthermore, with the exception of getting married and starting a family, it had been the last to-do on her life list.

Under the mistaken impression that falling in love would be just as easy as getting her MBA, Georgia had set about dating with the same sort of single-minded zeal she had with everything else. Though she abhorred exercise, she'd joined a gym, a hot spot of many young professionals. She'd want the future father of her children to be healthy, after all.

Next she'd enrolled in a couple continuing-education classes at the local university. A potential mate had to be smart. What better place to look?

Finally, for the sake of convenience, she'd joined

a couple of online dating sites, but after one horrible experience, she'd pulled her profile down from the site. When her single, mid-thirties, moderately attractive date had turned out to be a balding, married baby boomer in the throes of a midlife crisis, Georgia had deemed the online dating scene a bit too murky for her tastes.

She'd met Carter at a local upscale bistro on the heels of the online dating fiasco and had dubbed the "organic" meeting as a sign of good luck. She inwardly snorted. Looking back, he'd no doubt been hanging out there, looking for an easy mark. He'd been handsome, charming, witty, well-dressed and seemingly educated. Georgia sighed. She'd ignored that little prickle of intuition that had told her he wasn't the guy for her and soldiered on, determined to give him a chance.

Having listened to her mother and father rhapsodize their love-at-first-sight story, she believed— and despite the disastrous outcome of her efforts— *still* believed that when she found the man she was supposed to spend the rest of her life with, she'd *know.* Love wouldn't arrive on a gentle breeze, but would hurtle at her like a tsunami.

And it would have to, because she was through trolling, surfing, scouting and searching.

"I don't understand," Karen said, her brow knitting into a frown. "I thought you and Carter were through."

"We are."

"Then why are you and the bounty hunter looking for him?"

Georgia swallowed a sip of tea, wishing it was something stronger. "The bounty hunter is looking for him because he skipped bail. I'm looking for him because—" Georgia stopped, squeezed her eyes tightly shut, summoning the courage to go on.

Karen inhaled sharply and her eyes widened. "Ohmigod! You're pregnant, aren't you?"

"No!" Georgia told her, horrified. "I never slept with him, thank God."

Karen slumped and her expression became one of confusion. "Well if you aren't pregnant, then why would you be looking for him?"

"Because he took my mother's ring," she finally admitted, her throat tightening with emotion.

Once again Karen's eyes widened, first with shock, then with sympathy. "No," she breathed. She grabbed Georgia's hand, looking for the missing jewelry. "Oh, Georgia," she tutted. Her eyes blazed. "That *bastard*. I never liked him."

A total lie—Karen had been every bit as fooled by Carter as she had—but Georgia wasn't going to call her on it. What was the point? She related the details as she knew them to her friend and finished with the arrangement she'd made with Linc Stone.

She smiled wanly and pulled a shrug. "He's my only hope."

Karen grimaced and spun a mound of noodles onto her fork. "Sounds like you've pinned your hopes on an ass," she said grimly. "A decent guy would have helped you without you having to plan a free wedding for his little sister."

"I don't know," Georgia hedged, surprised at her gut reaction to defend him. It was desperation, she told herself, unwilling to examine her motives any further. "I think he's just used to working alone."

"Still, have a little compassion," Karen insisted doggedly, unwilling to let it go. "Sheesh. I hope he's good at what he does."

An image of Linc's disturbingly sexy face suddenly materialized in her mind's eye, causing a flutter of unwelcome, completely inappropriate heat to zigzag through her belly.

He certainly *looked* like he'd be good at what he does, Georgia thought, releasing a small sigh. Those keen green eyes didn't miss much and those muscles certainly hadn't gotten there by accident. He clearly worked hard at staying in shape, and she didn't get the impression that vanity wielded the whip prodding him to the gym. He didn't have that pretty-boy, let-me-shave-all-the-hair-off-my-body-so-that-you-can-see-how-big-my-muscles-are thing going on. Frankly, any man who was more meticulous about shaving his legs than she was got marked off her list. Talk about intimidating. Geez. She had enough body image issues to worry about without putting a hair competition into the mix.

No, like her, Linc Stone simply wanted to be the best—she'd recognized that too-familiar hunger the first time she'd seen him—and staying in shape was all part and parcel of being at the top of his game. And judging from those broad, muscled shoulders and sinfully ripped abs, anyone who tried to knock him off said game was in for one helluva fight. A little, surprisingly bloodthirsty thrill whipped its way through her at the mere thought, and she released a self-disgusted sigh. Hell, he wasn't her gladiator, for pity's sake. What was wrong with her? Was all that über-testosterone getting to her already?

Probably so, Georgia decided. Despite the fact that she should be exercising better sense and proper restraint—particularly in light of what had happened recently with Carter—Georgia couldn't seem to keep from thinking about Linc Stone. Imagining him naked, specifically. To say that she was attracted to him would be a mild understatement. She wanted to run her hands over his chest, kiss the underside of his jaw—taste the salty essence of his skin—and breathe naughty words into his ear. Simply looking at him made her entire body shimmer with need.

As for worrying about whether he was really good at what he did…Georgia wasn't. The police officer she'd first talked to after she'd realized what Carter had done had put her fears to rest. He'd taken one look at the file—at who had issued the bond specifically—and just smiled. "You're in luck, lady. AA Atco issued bail," he'd said. "Whether he knows it or not, your guy is as good as caught. Those Stone boys don't let *anyone* get away."

Georgia loaded *Dog, The Bounty Hunter* into her DVD player, snagged the remote control and determinedly settled in on her couch. Bogey and Bacall landed in her lap and Stitch curled in next to her hip, surrounding her with furry animal love.

Those Stone boys don't let anyone get away, she thought again.

Good, because that was precisely what she was counting on.

4

LINC WHEELED HIS midsize standard black SUV into a parking space outside Georgia's office and simply stared at the storefront, loath to go inside.

Weddings With Hart fell firmly into "girly" territory, and any man who entered her establishment no doubt had to check his balls at the door. Of course, if he was going into her store, then more than likely his fiancé had already confiscated the stones in question and carried them around in her purse for safe keeping. A droll smile rolled across his lips and he absently thumped the steering wheel with his thumb.

Just another reason he'd never tie the knot.

He liked his balls attached to his body, thank you very much, and the only reason he planned to go into this particular store this morning was because he'd agreed to pick her up here.

Big mistake, he realized now, his mouth going curiously dry. He should have met her at her house, or

made her come back over to the bond office. Coun-
terproductive, of course, because her office was the
logical place to start. Carter had liked doing his
business in Germantown—a trendy, moneyed area on
Memphis's front door—and most of the places they
were going to scope out today were here in this area.

Still... He couldn't shake a pervading sense of
doom, the sense that he was stepping into a mine-
field of sorts and one wrong move would leave him
shattered and broken.

Or worse, trapped, in a web made of tulle and a
shower of rice.

It was strange, Linc thought, because he'd never
worried about anything like this before. He'd always
been secure in the knowledge that he would remain
single. The idea that he was annoyed meant he felt
threatened and feeling threatened wasn't pleasant. In
fact, he hated it.

White twinkle lights wound through twisting
grapevines which had been strung around her windows and over her door. Dreaded tulle and lace
dripped like wedding cake frosting from the ceiling
and a luminous, frothy white dress with enough seed
pearls and sequins to make a girl giddy stood as the
perfect put-a-ring-on-my-finger-*now!* window dressing.

From his vantage point in the car, he could see

a lot of spindly-legged, gilded poofy furniture he was certain wouldn't support his weight, pale pink flowers, pink velvet and satin and tiny crystal chandeliers. It was like a wedding dollhouse, Linc thought with a snort. Designed as every girl's dream and every whipped guy's unwitting web of matrimonial hell. And the smiling bride in her gown was like an overdressed, big white spider waiting right smack-dab in the middle of it all.

He inwardly shuddered at the imagery and toyed with the idea of merely blowing the horn to alert her of his presence. He wouldn't, of course, because it was crass. Furthermore, though his word had been reluctantly given, it had been given all the same. He said he would help her and had agreed to pick her up here.

At the moment, he wasn't exactly sure which had been the less intelligent decision of the two, but he'd deal with it in a gentlemanly fashion all the same. Linc bared his teeth in a smile and exited his truck. Why would he do that?

Because he wouldn't let a little discomfort make a liar out of him.

The instant he opened the door, the intro to the "Wedding March" sounded, pushing his lips into a sneer of disgust. No doubt intended to bring a smile to a prospective bride's face, all Linc heard was *Doom, doom, do-doom. Doom, doom, do-doom.*

"Do you need some ointment for that?" a petite redhead with an unfortunate set of heavy freckles inquired with more sarcasm than solicitousness. She'd been seated behind a small, spindly legged desk when he walked in, but had stood.

Linc resisted the urge to bat at the wispy fabric hanging mere inches from his head and quirked a brow. "Come again?"

"Ointment," she repeated, smiling. She wore a name tag bearing the name Karen. "You know, for the hives you're about to break into."

"No, thank you," he said, hating that he was that damned transparent. He made an effort to appear normal, which curiously annoyed him even more. "I'm here for Georgia. Is she around?"

The redhead's eyes and mouth rounded simultaneously. "Oh," she breathed. "You must be the bounty hunter."

"Bond-enforcement agent, yes," he confirmed with a brisk nod. Bounty hunter was an outdated term, but one that hung around with irritating tenacity. Much like Karen, he decided uncharitably, which was hardly fair. It wasn't her fault he was in a bad mood.

"Right," she said. She cocked her head and gazed at him with blatant curiosity. "I'll let her know you're here."

He'd expected her to walk to the back, but instead she merely hollered in a singsongy kind of voice that instantly put him on edge. "Georgia, Mr. Stone's here for you." She smiled at him once more, crossed her arms expectantly over her chest and rocked back on her heels. "I'm sure she'll be out here in a minute."

The sooner the better, Linc thought, resisting the pressing urge to fidget. Badass bounty hunters *didn't* fidget, dammit. But between the intrigued I-know-something-that-you-don't smile on Karen's face and the proximity to all things 'til-death-do-us-part, Linc was beginning to feel a serious itch to turn tail and run coming on.

"Right on time," Georgia trilled, hurrying from the back.

For reasons beyond his immediate understanding, he felt a bolt of heat land in his groin, and a ridiculous smile try to take over his lips. With effort, he flattened his mouth. "Did you expect me to be late?"

Karen snorted and resumed her post behind the desk. "She expects everyone to be late. Don't take it personally. She typically builds fifteen minutes into every appointment to prevent 'downtime.'" She said "downtime" as though it were a dreaded, unforgivable sin. Irritating though she may be, Karen was proving to be quite a font of helpful information about his honorary assistant.

Linc's gaze slid to Georgia who looked ready to strangle her chatty help. He felt his traitorous lips twitch. "Is this true?"

She lifted her chin in a stubborn little angle he stupidly found sexy. "It's efficient."

He could certainly understand that. And she was nothing if not the perfect picture of efficiency. His moody gaze slid over her. Irritatingly, she'd pulled her beautiful hair up into that don't-touch-me ponytail again. Only the smallest hint of makeup tinted her face—it probably took her less than two to three minutes to apply, which was no doubt the point. Her clothes were tailored, high-end wrinkle resistant with little to no embellishments. Clean collar, flat-panel slacks, sleek jacket, no-nonsense shoes. Simple diamond studs winked in her ears and a nice watch glinted from her wrist. A slim leather bag—which he'd bet his left nut contained her cell phone, PDA and perfectly organized wallet—hung from her shoulder.

He was suddenly hit with the insane urge to pull down her hair, drag her tucked-in shirt from the waist-band of her pants—copping a feel in the process, of course, because he was a man—and throw a little dirt on her shoes. He wanted to mess her up a little. Rattle her cage and see what set her off.

Without warning a vision of setting her off in the

literal, biblical sense suddenly materialized in his mind's eye—*naked creamy skin, pouting rosy nipples, her perfectly straight teeth sinking into that plump lower lip as she came for him.* Linc simultaneously hardened and panicked, then gave his head a small shake to dislodge the vision. He blinked and, with difficultly, pulled the fully clothed version of Georgia Hart back into focus.

She'd definitely dressed for work, but not *his* kind of work. He reoutfitted her in formfitting black jeans, a black long-sleeved T-shirt, a pair of shit-kicker boots and backpack as opposed to the purse.

Ah, Linc thought. Much better. She'd never pull off fierce with that ultrafeminine face and curls, but *hot* was definitely doable.

In fact, insanely, she was hot now, otherwise he wouldn't be thinking about backing her against the wall and taking her until her eyes rolled back in her head.

"For future reference, I'm always on time. Is that what you're wearing?"

She looked down at herself, then her heavily lashed gaze bumped uncertainly back up to his. "It's what I have on. Is something wrong with it?"

"You don't look like a bond-enforcement agent."

"I didn't realize you wanted me to look like a bond-enforcement agent."

"For today it'll be fine," he said, purposely sounding skeptical. "Tomorrow you might want to wear something a little less dressy. If we have time today, we'll find you something." Actually, Linc thought, they would *make* time. If he had to have her along with him, he might as well amuse himself. And something about making Little Miss Prim and Proper dress for him was downright hysterical.

"I'm sure I've got something at home."

Karen, who'd been pretending not to be eavesdropping, snorted again.

"Does she have allergies?" Linc asked.

Georgia frowned darkly at her assistant. "She's only allergic to minding her own business."

"You made it my business when you made me sit through season three of *Dog, The Bounty Hunter* last night," Karen replied drolly, idly flipping through a bridal magazine.

Linc chuckled. "You watched that last night?"

Blushing furiously, Georgia muttered something ominous from between clenched teeth to her help before unhappily finding his gaze. She cleared her throat. "I thought it might be helpful."

"What? You couldn't find a book?"

"She found several," Karen piped up once more. She licked her thumb and idly flipped another page.

This time Linc didn't just chuckle, he laughed.

He passed a hand over his face, trying to wipe his smile away.

It didn't work.

"I don't understand what's so damned funny," Georgia snapped, walking around him toward the door. "I wanted to be prepared. You should be glad."

"Oh, I am," Linc said, trailing along behind her, smothering more laughter.

"You don't sound glad, you sound amused." She went unerringly to his SUV and waited for him to unlock and open the door.

"How did you know this was mine?"

"It's the same make and model Dog drives."

Linc felt his eyes widen and he drew up short. "The same make and model Dog—"

"Just kidding," she quipped, those dark eyes dancing with mischief. "I knew it was yours because I saw it when I came to your apartment. Your father had told me to look for it so I would know whether or not you were home and just hiding from me."

Linc paused, allowing that little infuriating tidbit to sink in. "Helpful fellow, my father, wasn't he?"

"Very accommodating," she said, smiling sweetly. He purposely invaded her personal space as he opened her door and had the pleasure of watching the smile falter. She smelled like strawberries and hay, Linc thought, equally intrigued and turned on. She pulled in a small breath and climbed inside.

"I wouldn't get used to that if I were you."

A genuine chuckle bubbled up her throat, pinging something deep inside him he instinctively knew he should ignore. "Oh, I'm not likely to make that mistake. You've been difficult, irritating, belligerent, rude and surly. Expecting you to be *accommodating* would stretch the limits of even my admittedly rubberized imagination."

He paused, unaccustomed to the company of a mouthy female. Gracie was mouthy, of course, but as his sister she didn't qualify. The women he ordinarily spent time with were more obliging. "Has anyone ever told you that you can be smart-ass?"

"My brother, but he doesn't count."

She had a brother? he thought, surprised. For whatever reason, he'd gotten the impression that she was completely alone. It had never occurred to him that she'd have any other family. She seemed so... self-sufficient. An island unto herself.

A thought struck. "Does he know the ring is missing?"

She flushed guiltily and bit her lip before responding. "Do you share your screwups with your family?"

His family was usually front-and-center with a bowl of popcorn in their laps and expectant faces when he screwed up, but he completely understood what she meant. "I guess that's a no." Linc shut her door, then rounded the hood and slid behind the wheel. "What are you going to do if you don't find it?"

Her jaw tightened and she fastened her seatbelt with a resolute click. "I *will* find it."

Her determination was admirable, but pushed the bounds of practicality. Odd when she seemed so grounded otherwise.

"But if you don't," he pressed, for whatever reason, feeling the need to prepare her for the worst. Hell, he wanted her to find the ring, as well, but she needed to be realistic. And the idea of having to comfort her when she came to the sad realization that the ring might be gone forever made him distinctly…uneasy.

"I'll just cross that bridge when I come to it, Mr. Stone," she said with a shaky breath.

Whatever, Linc thought grimly. So long as he didn't have to keep her from jumping off the damned thing, all would be fine.

"So I've made a list," Georgia said, trying to ignore the tantalizingly sexy length of denim-encased male leg mere inches from her own. Who would have thought a man's jean-clad thigh could be so damned sexy? Or that the air would thin to the point she felt light-headed the minute she got into close proximity with a put-upon bounty hunter with a chivalrous bone the size of a toothpick.

Linc grunted, seemingly unsurprised. "I would have been shocked if you hadn't." A smile tugged at the corner of his distractingly sensual mouth. "Of course, between cramming for Bounty Hunter 101 and watching all those episodes of *Dog,* I don't see how you've managed to find the time."

Georgia consulted her Palm Pilot and primly cleared her throat. "I got up early."

Not a total lie—she hadn't gone to bed at all. Between worrying about the ring and the looming rendezvous with a certain lethally good-looking bounty hunter, going to sleep simply hadn't been an option. Every time she'd started to doze off, she'd see her mother's ring on *his* finger, of all places.

Clearly her subconscious had gone off the deep end because she suspected getting a ring of any sort—much less of the happily-ever-after variety— onto Linc Stone's finger was not only a lost cause, but an act of sheer stupidity destined for ultimate heartbreak.

Despite making the disastrous and costly mistake with Carter, Georgia could generally read a guy pretty accurately when it came to matters of the heart. For instance, she could usually tell when they were getting married because they were afraid of losing their current love, were getting married because "the time had come" and they were being pressured by their intended and families, whether a guy was going to be a cheating bastard, or if he truly wanted to spend the rest of his life with the woman he'd proposed to.

Sadly, those were getting fewer and far between.

While Linc Stone didn't necessarily fall into any of those categories, it didn't take a look from behind the Hubble Telescope to see that he had "commitment-phobic" written all over him.

The eternal question, of course, was...why? Previous heartbreak? she wondered speculatively, darting him a look from the corner of her eye. Or was it something else? For whatever reason, she got the impression it was something else. Intuition told her he'd never been close enough to another person to have ever allowed the initial heartbreak to start with.

Surely he realized that his reticence to settle down with one particular woman put a big, fat bull's-eye on his forehead, Georgia thought, smiling wryly. Particularly to those of the competitive variety. Typically she lumped herself into that category, but she knew a lost cause when she saw one. She imagined Linc was good for a fun date and a night of sheet-

scorching sex, but only an idiot would expect anything more out of him.

And, despite recent evidence to the contrary, she
was no idiot.

Furthermore, she didn't have time for fun and,
while a night of sheet-scorching sex would be nice,
something told her she'd get burned in more ways
than one. All of this was assuming, of course, that
he'd be interested in her to start with. Georgia gave
a mental eye-roll.

When pigs flew.

Guys like Linc Stone didn't give her the time of
day. They never had.

Part of what made Georgia a good wedding planner
was the sad fact that she wasn't competition for the potential bride. She was passably attractive, but not
gorgeous. She owned a mirror and had no illusions
about her body. She'd always carried around an extra
fifteen pounds on her petite frame which, while it
hadn't made her pleasantly plump, had made her
curvier than what was presently considered fash-
ionable.

Frankly, she'd always enjoyed food too much to
worry over the additional weight, and so long as her
clothes fit well she didn't plan on going on a diet.
She'd leave starving to the beautiful people, thank
you, and be content with the body she inhabited. Was

it perfect? Not by any stretch of the imagination. Her breasts were a little on the smallish side, her thighs and butt a little too padded, but thanks to Victoria's Secret and slimming slacks she could disguise the majority of her—she cast a covert glance at her chest—shortcomings.

To be perfectly honest, until her second year of college she'd never really noticed a lack of interest from the "sexy boys." She'd always been too busy studying for the next exam or working at her father's business. She'd refused to allow her parents to simply pay for her school and had worked off at least part of the difference at Hart Industries.

Her dad had always joked that she'd been too much like him, had told her that he'd worked hard for his family's benefit, but having seen one too many spoiled rich kids pitch a tantrum over their new BMW being the wrong color, Georgia just couldn't let her father foot the entire bill. Just because he'd worked hard didn't mean that she didn't have to. It was a work ethic she and her brother shared, much to their parents' pride, she knew.

At any rate, though she hadn't done it purposely, she'd managed to avoid the whole find-a-boyfriend frenzy that her other counterparts were rabidly participating in at the time.

Then it had happened.

She'd been seated in the Student Union Building, cramming a French fry into her mouth and Advanced Business Principles into her brain, when she'd caught sight of him from across the room.

Mitch Mullins, a blond Adonis track star with a killer smile and abs that would make a girl's knees weak. One look at this gorgeous specimen of man had awakened every dormant sexual cell in her body. She'd gone from bud to full bloom in an instant, had become a stranger in her own body. She'd wandered around in lust for weeks, finally mustered the courage to walk across an off-campus restaurant to talk to him, only to have the clueless ass mistake her for the waitress.

She'd been mortified.

Furthermore, it had only taken one disinterested look from him to make her realize that she simply didn't register on his radar as a woman. She might as well have been genderless.

Because Georgia liked to take the scientific and thorough approach to most everything, she tested her theory with other gorgeous guys around school. She could be their friend, she could be their tutor, she could proof their papers and help locate books in the library—the one thing she could not do was pique their interest.

Initially this conclusion had been quite heart-breaking, but once she'd gotten past the preliminary sting her legendary practicality had surfaced. Just because the gorgeous guys didn't notice her didn't mean that she didn't have anything to offer or to bring to a relationship. It simply meant that they were superficial and shallow and who'd want to date a guy like that anyway?

In other words, *she* was not the problem.

Once that revelation had set in it had really freed her up to other possibilities. She'd stopped looking at traditionally good-looking men and had opted for compelling and smart instead. Though she could honestly say she'd never been head over heels in love, she'd developed a strong attachment to a guy in grad school and, ultimately, he'd been her first.

Considering the fact that her ripening hormones had been wreaking havoc for almost a year, Georgia had expected more from her initial experience. While it hadn't been completely lacking, she'd always sensed—and still did despite having a couple of other lovers—that there was…more. More of what she wasn't exactly certain, but she suspected it all the same.

Her gaze slid to the man seated next to her and she felt the tops of her thighs burn.

No doubt he could give a girl more, Georgia thought, her mouth instantly parching. Everything about Linc Stone exuded confidence and sexual superiority. It wasn't just nice bone structure and a wicked smile, the heavy-lidded, I've-got-a-perpetual-secret, sleepy-looking gaze or even the distractingly sexy curls brushing his collar, though admittedly, that was enough.

Linc Stone had that indefinable something, that rare "it" quality that made a girl squirm for no reason, sigh with longing and yearn for the merest touch from his talented hands. Georgia instinctively knew that a single stroke of his knuckles across her cheek would elicit enough heat in her blood to set her panties on fire.

That was the more she was missing.

And *that* was the more she'd just as soon forget about, particularly with him.

Linc chose that moment to look at her and those compelling green orbs sucked the air right out of her lungs, leaving her momentarily breathless. And brainless apparently, she thought, feeling her lips slide into an embarrassed smile. Hell, it wasn't like he could read her mind.

The corner of his mouth hitched into an almost smile. Odd how potent that half grin could be. "Okay, Ms. List Maker. Where to first?"

Hell, Georgia thought miserably. I'm going to

hell. Because if he so much as crooked his finger, she knew she'd be a goner.

With effort, she managed to focus. "I met him at Marcello's over in English Village. He seemed to be a regular there. I thought we should try there first."

Linc snorted and slipped the gearshift into reverse. "Figures."

"What do you mean?"

"If a man goes into that chick haunt, then he's not there to get a chocolate-swirl-raisin-currant-date-nut-gluten-free bagel, sweetheart. He's trolling."

Come to think of it, she rarely saw any men in Marcello's and if they were, they were generally accompanied by a woman. Strictly speaking, it did cater to more of a female clientele. Annoyed with herself for not realizing this to start with, Georgia gritted her teeth and opted to argue. Why? Who knew? But she couldn't seem to help herself. "Are you saying men don't eat bagels?"

He flashed her a smile. "Only at home. Behind a locked door. In the dark."

"Marcello's sells a wonderful prune Danish. You should try one," she suggested.

He grimaced, almost comically. "Why would I want to do that?"

Georgia grinned pointedly at him. "Because you are obviously full of shit."

Rather than being offended, he chuckled, the sound deep and curiously soothing. "Nicely done," he told her. "I didn't see that coming."

"Probably a carrot muffin would do you some good, as well."

He pulled out onto Union Avenue and hung a right. "Too bad they don't have anything to cure your problem." A dark chuckle broke up in his throat. "We'd need a fifth of Jack Daniel's, a pair of needle-nosed pliers and a Shop-Vac for that."

Needle-nosed pliers and a Shop-Vac? Georgia thought, equally startled and intrigued. What the— "I'm not even going to ask," she said, pretending to be unconcerned.

Linc chuckled again. "I figured as much." He slid her another one of those sly looks. "But you want to."

Perfect, Georgia thought. He wasn't just gorgeous, he was a gorgeous know-it-all. "You're right," she admitted, hating herself. "I do. So tell me."

He laughed, the gorgeous wretch. "The Jack would loosen you up. I'd need the Shop-Vac to suck the stick outta your ass and the needle-nose pliers to remove the splinters."

"Clever," Georgia said, smirking. She decided a subject change was in order. "How much time are you devoting to this today?"

"All of it," Linc told her. His jaw flexed with grim determination. "You're getting every minute of my time until we find Carter Watkins."

"E-every minute?" she asked, curiously intimidated by Linc's revelation.

He sighed and pulled the truck into the English Village parking lot. "Every last one."

She should have been thrilled—the sooner they found Carter the sooner she could get the ring back—and having Linc's unwavering attention and time on this case was definitely to her advantage. Logical, rational, reasonable.

She should have been thrilled…and yet she wasn't.

More like unnerved. Being around Linc Stone, given this unfortunate sex-tingling, nipple-hardening attraction for small periods of time, was going to be difficult enough, but at least she'd thought she'd get a break. She'd retreat, regroup, possibly masturbate to take the edge off, then she'd be ready to deal with him. Prolonged exposure to his sex appeal, on the other hand, would be damned dangerous.

"Come on," he said. "Let's go kick some ass."

5

"KICK SOME ASS?" Georgia parroted, seemingly alarmed. Linc smothered a smile as she scrambled out the truck and fell in step beside him. "You're kidding, right? We can't kick ass at Marcello's. I'm a regular."

"Good. That'll work to our advantage." He drew up short right as he neared the door. "A few ground rules. I'm in charge, follow my lead—that one's important—and don't tell anyone why we're really looking for Carter. Understood?"

Though he could tell she wanted to argue, she nodded. Good, he thought. Better that she learn now that he was boss. "You said you met Carter here. Did you come here together often beyond that?"

"A few times."

"Would the staff recognize him? Know who he was?"

"They should."

"Good. You're trying to reach him because he's

left some things at your place and you've only just now found them."

"But—"

"Do you have any business cards?"

"Yes, but—"

"Give them one. Ask them to call you if he comes in. Got it? Okay, we're good. Let's roll." Before she could toss another "but" at him, he opened the door and gently nudged her inside.

She shot him a glare over her shoulder. She was too damned cute to carry the look off, but he instinctively knew he'd pay for her displeasure at some point. She might look sweet, but given the sheer determination and mouthiness he'd endured since meeting her, he knew better than to expect anything different.

"Good morning, Georgia," a cheerful clerk said from behind the counter. "The usual?"

So they knew her well then, Linc decided. That definitely worked in their favor.

"Yeah, and I'd like to add a prune Danish for my friend here." She jerked her head in his direction and made a false moue of sympathy. "He's having a little plumbing problem, if you know what I mean," she stage-whispered loud enough for everyone in the restaurant to hear.

Linc felt his cheeks burn and he managed a pained smile. "I don't need one, thanks."

"Would you prefer bran?" she asked delicately.

"I don't need anything."

"Don't be silly," Georgia said briskly. "We all have that problem from time to time." She cleared her throat. "Speaking of problems, Mandy…Carter hasn't happened to have been in recently, has he?"

Well done, Linc thought. Very smooth, very casual.

Mandy's uncertain gaze bounced between him and Georgia, as though she didn't quite know what to make of Georgia asking about the old boyfriend in front of who she assumed was the new one. "You mean that guy you used to date?"

"That'd be the one," she confirmed grimly.

Mandy's brow wrinkled in thought for a few seconds, then she shook her head. "He hasn't come in on my shift," she finally said. "You might check with the evening staff."

Georgia winced with disappointment. "He left a couple of things at my place that I need to get back to him and I haven't had any luck reaching him." She reached into her purse and withdrew a slim silver card holder. "Would you mind taking my card and giving me a call if he comes in?"

Mandy nodded. "Sure."

"And don't let him know," Georgia added, rocking back on her heels and looking all mysterious. "I want to surprise him."

A slow, knowing smile dawned over Mandy's lips, indicating that they'd just formed one of those odd womanly bonds only chicks understood. Women, Linc thought with a mental snort of derision.

"You betcha," she said.

Georgia accepted the trendy foil bag which held their breakfast and her coffee drink. It was one of those double-espresso-mocha-latte-half-half-decaf things he abhorred. He took his coffee black. The end. In his opinion, everything else was nonsense. Furthermore, who had the time to stand around and wait on coffee? He had an automatic timer on his machine which brewed it for him before he ever got out of bed. Now that, by God, was what he called efficient.

"What would you like to drink?" Mandy asked him.

Georgia winced. "You should probably have some sort of juice, don't you think?"

He would get her back for this, Linc decided, looking into those deceptively sweet brown eyes. He would *so* get her back. "I'll have coffee," he said, smiling over gritted teeth. "Plain, black coffee."

A minute later they were back in his truck, heading to destination number two on her list— Gib's Ribs, another trendy bistro where Carter could sit and look important without having to spend any money. Georgia, looking particularly pleased with herself, tore a chunk from her poppy-seed muffin and popped it into her mouth. Despite being royally irritated, there was something disturbingly erotic about watching her eat.

It was her mouth, he decided broodingly.

It was full and lush, ripe like a strawberry and though he never tasted it—and didn't intend to—would no doubt be just as sweet. He immediately imagined it sliding down his chest, then wrapping around that throbbing part of him that didn't seem to recognize she was a threat. He hardened again and mentally swore.

"Is something wrong?" Georgia asked, pausing guardedly.

"No."

"Do you want your prune Danish?"

In answer to that question, he chucked the entire bag out the window.

She gasped, horrified. "You just littered!"

"There'll be a convict along directly to pick it up." One of his father's politically incorrect lines and frankly, he hated it, but he wasn't about to give her the satisfaction of being right. Even though she was, dammit. He hated that he'd allowed her to irritate him so damned much, but he didn't seem to be able to control himself. Which was precisely why he'd tried so desperately to avoid her.

He knew—*knew*—that she'd be trouble.

He didn't litter, dammit. He'd cleaned all of the empty soda cans and garbage out of his vehicle this morning just so that she could get in it.

Georgia pulled her cell phone from her purse and idly keyed in a number.

"Who are you calling?" he asked suspiciously.

"The police. I'm going to report you."

He blinked, astounded, and felt his jaw drop. "Have you forgotten that I'm doing you a favor?"

"Have you forgotten the law?" she shot back. "Whatever happened to 'Sworn to protect and serve'?"

"That's the police," he growled, making a grab for her phone.

She leaned out of his way. "Whatever. You back up the police, don't you? What sort of example are you setting? You're supposed to be an example to the community."

Her penchant for being right was becoming a perpetual thorn in his side. "I'm a bond-enforcement agent, Pollyanna, not a civil servant." Good grief, it wasn't like he'd run over a puppy. It was a foil bag.

"You're a litterer. And litterers get hefty fines." She perked up and leaned even farther away from him as someone evidently picked up on the other end of the line.

Motherfuc—

"Ah, yes. My name is Georgia Hart and I'd like to report a crime."

Geez, God. How freaking humiliating. Aside from making him look bad, he'd get razzed for this unmercifully by every one of his law-enforcement buddies. Not to mention his family. Cade, in particular. There was only one thing he could do.

"Yes, a crime. I know the perpetrator and will be willing to fill out a sworn statement." She shot him a smug look.

Because his brain had been replaced with an irrational mass of anger, Linc broke another law and committed an abrupt U-turn. She squealed in alarm and her organized purse, muffin and coffee went flying. "I'll go back," he said, feeling his belly swell with galling dread. He took advantage of gravity and snatched the cell phone out of her hand as she landed hard against him. Any other time he would have appreciated having a soft female plastered against him, the feel of a plump breast landing against his arm, but at the moment he was too irritated.

He snapped her phone shut, effectively ending the call. "God, woman, you are a lot of trouble," he said, hoping his exasperation covered the shake in his voice.

She straightened herself, primly smoothed her hair making sure every last strand was still firmly snug against her head. "You should have more respect for the law."

He shot her a pointed look. "You should have more respect for someone doing you a favor."

She opened her mouth, prepared to argue, but ultimately snapped it shut. She swore softly under her breath—a surprisingly harsh epithet out of that sweet-looking mouth—and released a pent-up sigh. "You're right. I apologize."

He didn't know what surprised him more—the fact that she admitted she was wrong, or the apology. Both issued from a woman were out of the realm of his experience. Not that he'd ever argued with a woman the way he did with her. Honestly, Georgia Hart was in a league of her own when it came to pushing his buttons and making him feel like he needed to take the world apart a piece at a time. All of that combined with that annoyingly sexy mouth he couldn't seem to stop looking at, the incessant need he'd suddenly developed to land between her thighs, and Linc was ready to howl.

Ultimately, though, he'd suddenly realized something much more profound and shaming than he'd bargained for from her—this little mouthy wedding planner with the wounded, sweet brown eyes, sexy mouth and too-tight ponytail had more character than he did.

He pulled off to the side of the road, got out of his truck, snagged the bag and climbed back in behind the wheel. His gaze drifted to Georgia who was trying to repair some of the damage his U-turn had wrought. Coffee stained her white blouse and muffin crumbs were all over her black suit. Though she hadn't uttered a single complaint, he knew it was killing her. Feeling even more like an ass, Linc cleared his throat. "You'll need to change."

"I will."

"Good, I wanted to take you shopping for proper bounty-hunter clothes, anyway." He put the truck back in gear and merged with traffic.

She stopped putting things in her purse long enough to glare at him. "I don't want to go shopping," she said, her voice vibrating with irritation. "I want to go home, clean up and change clothes."

Linc started to argue, but ultimately changed his mind. A thought struck and he hit Send on her cell phone, redialing the last number she'd called.

"Weddings With Hart, this is Karen. How can I help you?"

He chuckled grimly and shook his head, then shot her an appraising look. "You're slick, Georgia, I'll give you that."

She merely smiled.

Another blanket of heat blasted him and he resisted the urge to lean forward and taste those strawberry lips. He wanted to feel her, Linc thought. Mold his hands over her face and know her shape. Every last covered up, pinned down inch.

Slick and had character, Linc thought, staring at her mouth once again.

Now that was a dangerous combination.

JAW TIGHT AND EVERY MUSCLE seemingly clenched in uncomfortable misery—it was her talent, after all, Georgia thought morosely—Linc wheeled his SUV down her long paved drive. Other than to gruffly ask if the coffee had burned her, he hadn't had much to say. It hadn't—luckily the majority of it had landed on his dashboard—but she was still stupidly touched that he'd asked. He might be a perpetual frat-boy ogre, but he'd at least demonstrated a modicum of rudimentary courtesy.

Live oaks and sugar maples dressed in their latest fall colors, along with an occasional cypress to break up the monotony, dotted the rolling landscape. A sturdy split rail fence marched along the drive and separated various pastures, and the big red barn she'd always fancifully considered the castle for their horses sat in the distance, a postcard image for lazy summer days and the smell of sweet hay. Several horses munched on the rare clump of lingering green grass, her blue roan mare, Magalina—Mags for short—included.

"You ride?" he asked, seemingly surprised. Those deep green orbs had widened with interest and, dare she hope…appreciation?

No doubt he thought the pastime was too dirty a hobby for her. She rather liked the idea of shattering one of his perceptions about her. "I'm not going to win any awards, but yes." She pointed to Mags. "That mare is mine."

He whistled low under his breath. "She's pretty. What's her name?"

"Magalina."

A short chuckle burst from his throat. "Magalina? As in Magalina Hagalina? The old children's song about the ugly girl?"

Georgia smiled. "That'd be the one."

He poked his tongue in his cheek. "Why would you name that beautiful animal after an ugly girl?"

"I didn't want her getting too full of herself."

Again another startled chuckle rumbled up from his chest and he turned to stare at her. "You're kidding, right?"

Georgia smiled and rolled her eyes. "Of course, I'm kidding. I didn't name her. Her previous owners did. She wasn't so beautiful when she was a colt. She looked like she'd rolled around in a puddle of ink. Her confirmation was a little off—legs too short and she was awkwardly gaited."

Linc slowed and watched Mags canter in perfect form across the field. "Looks like she's past that."

"She is. She just needed a little time to grow and come into her own. Her owners were too impatient." She pulled a shrug. "Their loss, my gain."

"I can't argue with you there."

Georgia felt a droll smile roll across her lips. "Well, there's got to be a first time for everything."

Smiling, Linc slid her a considering glance. "You're just not going to miss an opportunity, are you?"

She pulled another small, hopeless shrug. "I can't seem to help myself."

And it was true. In her profession there'd been times she'd not only had to bite her tongue, but resist the urge to gnaw if off completely. She'd mastered the delicate balance of being both courteous and firm, of orchestrating the perfect compromise. Why, then, couldn't she keep her uncharitable comments to herself when it came to Linc Stone? Why did she want to goad him at every turn? Annoy him? Particularly when, as he'd so irritatingly pointed out, he was doing her a favor?

Ordinarily she was pretty good at protecting her own interests, but with Linc, logic seemed to fly out the window. Much like the Danish he'd tossed earlier, Georgia thought, smothering a laugh. Honestly, she'd been completely shocked and outraged over his littering, but somehow knowing that she'd pushed him out of character as well made her feel marginally better.

In other words, she wasn't the only one getting knocked off their game.

Linc slowed once more. "Is this your place?"

"No, that's my brother's. We both moved into the house after my parents died, but I've since built a place farther back on the property," she said. "Just follow the bend in the road."

Linc hummed under his breath and continued on around the corner. "That's it?" he asked, seemingly surprised once more, as her house came into view.

Georgia smiled. "That's it."

"It's not what I expected."

She could certainly understand that. Given the enormous stately Colonial—complete with the circular drive and fountain—her parents had built, Georgia's modest two-story farmhouse seemed curiously misplaced on the Hart Estate. Even Jack had been a bit surprised when she'd shown him her house plans.

"Just pull around back," Georgia told him, pointing to the carport at the rear of the house. Yellow mums and purple pansies bloomed from big barrels placed on either side of the drive and a flag bearing the phrase "Home Sweet Home" swung in the gentle fall breeze. Eclectic bird feeders and baths we're strewn around her brick patio and a freestanding fireplace took center stage, her comfortable old wicker rockers planted in front of it for optimal warming pleasure.

Linc, she noticed, took every bit of this in stride…until he saw her antique claw-foot tub. She knew that it was a bit startling, but she loved it. It was the ultimate indulgence, complete with hot water and bubble bath.

Smiling, he chewed the corner of his lip and quirked a brow. "You take a bath in that? Out here?"

"There's an alarm at the entrance of my driveway," Georgia told him. "It gives me time to make myself presentable." Or scurry inside, as the case may be. Typically, the only people who came to visit were Karen or Jack, and those visits weren't often when she was bathing.

Linc shook his head, seemingly impressed, and shifted into park. He climbed out of the truck and followed her inside. Bogey and Bacall lounged on the rug in front of the kitchen sink and Stitch came running across the hardwood, his nails clipping a steady beat along with his excited bark. Though he normally growled at strangers, the tiny black dog merely stared at Linc, sizing him up.

Linc bent down and offered his hand, allowing the dog to give him a tentative sniff. "I'm guessing there's a good reason your dog is wearing a diaper."

Georgia smiled. "He's wearing a diaper because he has bladder issues and I don't want him peeing all over the house while I'm gone."

He nodded, his lips twitching. "Reason enough."

"I got him at the shelter," Georgia told him. "He'd been mistreated. Kicked repeatedly according to my vet," she said, anger making her voice shake.

"Damn."

"I know." She nodded at the cats. "They're rescues, as well." She'd save them all if she had the time and room, Georgia thought, but at least this way she felt like she was doing something to help a few. Make their lives a little better. Too often people acquired animals, then didn't want to keep up the responsibility and maintenance the animals required.

Having gotten Stitch's stamp of approval, Linc stood and glanced around the room. "This is nice," he said.

Though it was technically the left butt-cheek of the house, in the figurative sense it was most definitely the heart. Despite the fact they lived separate busy lives, Jack usually joined her for dinner a couple of times a week.

Since her tastes leaned toward a French-country style, she'd painted the walls a rich buttery cream, and her cabinets were a substantial and heavy design, finished in cool maple with a deep mocha glaze. The effect was subtle but significant, giving them an aged appearance. Lavender bloomed from her windowsill, sleek toasted-almond granite served as her countertops, and a copper sink and range hood—the crown jewels of her kitchen—completed the look. Her grandmother's antique trestle table rounded out the decor. A bowl, much like the one she'd seen in Linc's loft, sat in the middle of the table. He smiled when he saw it and cast her an un-readable look.

"I noticed some similar pottery at your house," she said. "I bought it downtown. Looks like it could be from the same artist, doesn't it?"

He merely nodded, silently agreeing with her.

At any rate, she'd spent a king's ransom on the kitchen, but wouldn't change a thing. It was her favorite room in the house.

"Wow," Linc said, eyeing the pot rack over her island. "This is amazing."

"Thank you," Georgia murmured, pleased and

curiously relieved. It shouldn't matter if he approved of her house or not, yet for reasons beyond her immediate understanding…it did. "The living room is through here," she said, directing him past the dining room. "You're welcome to wait here while I clean up and change."

"Sure," he said, shoving his hands in his pockets. "Do you mind if I wander around down here and look around while you get ready?"

Her foot on the first tread of the stairs, Georgia stopped. "Er…I guess not."

She didn't have any idea what he expected to find, but if he wanted to check things out she really couldn't think of a legitimate objection.

"Architecture is a bit of a hobby of mine." He looked around and smiled a bit uncertainly, as though a memory were hovering just out of reach. "This house reminds me of something I've seen before, but I can't quite put my finger on it. It's bugging the hell out of me."

Georgia smiled and pointed to a print on her wall. "Take a look at that picture over there and see if it jogs your memory." Though she should have gone on upstairs, she waited instead for his reaction.

"Well, I'll be damned," he breathed, staring at an original print of her home from a Sears Roebuck catalog. "I knew I had seen it before." He turned and his equally astonished and impressed gaze tangled with hers. "A kit house?"

"The Chelsea," she replied. "With a few modern modifications, of course. The original only had one bathroom and virtually no closet space. I had to rearrange a few little things, but the overall layout is the same."

He passed a hand over his face and inspected the print once more. "What on earth led you to do something like this?"

"It was my grandparents' home. It burned shortly after I graduated from college." She lifted her shoulders in a small shrug. "I wanted it back."

Linc's mossy green gaze caught and held hers again, sucking the air out of the room. A small smile played around his lips, as though he wasn't quite sure what to make of her. "This is bad. You're not staying in the box."

She blinked. "What?"

"You're not staying in the box I put you in." He shoved his hands into his pockets. "I'd pegged you for a tidy patio home with little to no grass for minimum lawn management, trendy chrome appliances and sleek modern no-fuss furniture. Instead you've got acres of yard, a claw-foot tub *outside*—where you bathe *naked*—and a period replica house that couldn't be further from a patio home than an Airstream travel trailer." He poked his tongue in his cheek and shook his head. "Like I said, you're not staying in the box."

Ridiculously pleased at the backhanded compliment, Georgia returned his grin. "Then maybe you shouldn't try to pigeonhole people."

6

PIGEONHOLING HER certainly wasn't working out for
him, Linc thought, hours later as they ordered dinner
at their last stop of the evening. They'd canvassed a
good bit of ground today and hadn't gotten so much
as a kernel of useful information. Either Carter
Watkins had left town, was lying incredibly low, or
had moved his scam to another part of the city.

Linc knew it was particularly distressing for Georgia, but like he'd told her only a few minutes ago, a
lead could turn up where they least expected it. Sometimes he'd go out to look for a skip and hit pay dirt
on the first try. Other times—he pulled a mental
shrug—he'd be a gnat's ass away from throwing in
the towel, and a lucky break would come his way.

Either way they would find him, he thought determinedly. Whether or not they found the ring along
with him remained to be seen, but they'd simply
have to deal with that when the time came. For her
sake, he hoped luck would be in her favor. Unfortu-

nately—stupidly—any other scenario that didn't result in her happiness made his stomach cramp and his insides twist with dread.

Not good, he knew. He'd allowed himself to get entirely too invested in her problem, but at this point wasn't sure how to make it stop. Frankly, though he liked to think he'd been in control of this situation, Linc knew better.

Hell, he'd lost control the minute she'd come knocking on his door. Possibly even sooner.

Furthermore, the more he learned about Georgia Hart, the more he liked her. That was a novel experience in and of itself. Linc typically didn't like women one way or another. He lusted, he enjoyed their physical company, he cut them loose. Game over. *Liking* one was so far removed from his area of expertise he didn't know quite what to make of it.

But he did know this—the sooner he found Carter and escorted her out of his immediate vicinity the better. Otherwise he feared he'd do something even more ignorant, like try to seduce her.

Aside from being thoroughly provoking, he was also finding her increasingly harder to resist. He wanted to touch her, taste her, sample every delectable portion of her body, which was ridiculous when ultimately, she shouldn't be his type. She was a friggin' wedding planner for chrissakes. His worst nightmare. She believed in true love and happy endings, in holding hands and pillow talk, all of which made him break out in an invisible rash.

But when he looked at her…

Linc released a breath and covertly watched her from across the table. When he looked at her, something shifted in his chest and then a blast of need would broadside him, knocking every bit of reservation from his brain. His dick ached, his fingers tingled, his mouth watered.

When they'd gone back to her house this morning, Linc had fully expected her to change into another outfit identical to the one she'd had on. Instead, just to prove him wrong, he suspected, she'd come downstairs in a clingy black sweater, black jeans and tall, black leather boots. They weren't the shit-kickers he'd imagined, but the wedge heel gave her a little added height and a swing to her walk that had made the beast in him howl with approval. Linc released a pent-up breath.

In fact, he didn't know what he expected, but the full, heart-shaped, luscious bottom that filled out those jeans and that tiny waist sure as hell hadn't been it. He felt his dick stir just thinking about it, then felt it harden further imagining it naked and wet, settled outside in that hedonistic bathtub.

Linc was rarely, if ever, surprised, but learning that little tidbit...now that had been a shocker.

While he might have been able to read Georgia's predicament and mood the first time he'd met her, he clearly hadn't pegged her right. Odd for him, but he supposed it could happen. If anyone would have told him that the type A wedding planner—who was so friggin' anal she was currently eating her food a section at a time from her plate—would commune naked with nature in an outdoor bathtub, he would have told them to kiss his ass. The fact that she was brave enough—hell, cool and confident enough—to do it impressed him beyond measure. He could see her there, Linc thought, his gaze turning inward.

Dark curly hair hanging over the end of the tub as she sank beneath the steaming water, a sigh leaking out of those beautiful lips, lids fluttered shut, her breasts plump and pale in the moonlight...

Linc let go a shaky breath. Box, hell, he thought. She'd *obliterated* the box.

Georgia ended another call from Karen, carefully walking her through another averted disaster. Honestly, her assistant needed constant assistance.

"Sorry about that," Georgia said. "She's not used to being on her own."

Linc spooned up a bite of beef stew. "Is she capable of handling it without you?"

"She is. She just doesn't like to." A self-deprecating smile curved her ripe lips. "As you might have noticed, I'm a bit particular."

"You?" he gasped, feigning surprise. "Surely you're kidding. Surely working with you is a cakewalk."

"Hey," she teased. "I noticed you've fielded quite a few phone calls today, as well."

It was true, Linc had to admit. Not so much on skips and stuff, but rather the whole True Blue Bail Bonds issue. Georgia had caught enough of his one-sided conversation to know that they were having problems. To give her credit, she'd merely quirked an inquiring brow, but hadn't tried to pry. He honestly didn't know what he was going to do about the situation. Advertising cost a fortune and since their business was taking a revenue hit, funds were at an all-time low. Talk about a catch-22. This was definitely one of those it-takes-money-to-make-money sort of predicaments.

"Here's the difference," Linc finally told her. "Your help will work, she's just afraid of you because you're so demanding."

"Particular," Georgia corrected, smiling from behind her tea glass. "I'm *particular.*"

"Whatever. Anyway, my point is…my help just doesn't want to deal with it." He laughed. "I'm the one with the college education, ergo, I must be the one to handle it."

She pursed her lips and cocked her head. "Makes sense to me."

"Hello?" Linc reminded her again, feigning outrage. "Have you forgotten about the favor? You're supposed to take my side. Honestly, woman," he chided, tempering the criticism with a smile. "Is the significance of loyalty completely lost on you?"

She chuckled, the sound soft and feminine in their little darkened corner of the restaurant. At some point during the day her ponytail had started sagging and she hadn't bothered to fix it. While no curls had officially come loose, the relaxed version of the hairdo was much better. A current of heat landed in his loins, once again forcing him to shift in his seat.

"Just because you're doing me a favor doesn't mean that I have to take your side." Having finished with her mashed potatoes, she speared a piece of steamed broccoli and popped it in her mouth. "Furthermore, your favor wasn't free, remember? I'm doing you one, as well."

And there was that, Linc thought, once again finding himself on the wrong end of right. He shrugged. "Semantics."

Georgia rolled her eyes, but didn't argue. "What's your degree in?"

"Criminal justice."

"That's apt, I suppose."

"It helps," Linc admitted. "Honestly, it was more important to Dad and Cade, my brother, that I go to college than it ever was to me. I always knew I'd go into the family business."

She took another sip of tea. "Maybe they wanted you to have something to fall back on if something went wrong with the family business."

He chuckled darkly. "If that was the case, then I should have been an art major."

Georgia's eyes lit with intrigue, swiftly followed by surprise borne of sudden insight. "The pottery," she breathed. "Those are your pieces, aren't they? That's why you smiled when you saw my bowl."

"They are," he admitted, pleased that she'd liked his work enough to purchase of piece of it. He'd been secretly startled and damned pleased to see one of his bowls on her kitchen table. Though she'd only been inside his house for a few minutes, he should have realized that she would have noticed them. Like him, she paid attention to everything.

"It's beautiful work, Linc," she said, a hint of gratifying admiration in her gaze. She gave a little self-deprecating laugh. "Well, you know I like it. I've got more of it upstairs, a bluish-green floor vase in my bedroom."

Linc nodded. He remembered the piece she was talking about. He'd been especially proud of it. It had a very sensual feel to it—smooth and rounded with very erotic lines. Perfect art for the bedroom, he decided, his moody gaze finding hers.

"I bought it at Lucinda's downtown," she said.

"Lucinda's always been very supportive of my work."

"Have you had a gallery showing yet?"

"In May," Linc said, feeling his chest inflate with pride. "I'm working on a collection now."

Georgia nodded, seemingly impressed. "My only foray into pottery was a clumpy paperweight I made at summer camp one year." She paused, a question in her gaze. "So…how does a bounty hunter become interested in pottery?"

Linc chuckled under his breath. "It's a bit of a stretch, isn't it?"

"It's different," she admitted, cocking her head.

"My mom," Linc told her, chasing a bead of moisture down the side of his beer bottle with his finger. "She had a wheel out in our barn. She used to go out there in the evenings, throw pots to keep from cracking our heads, I imagine," he said, chuckling. "After she died, I started playing around with it and discovered that I enjoyed it, as well. The feel of the clay beneath my hands, molding and shaping it into form. It was very therapeutic." His gaze knotted with hers. "And the rest, as they say, is history."

Georgia nodded, then blinked drunkenly, her gaze drifting over his hands. She cleared her throat. "What about the guitar? It looked well-loved."

Linc shrugged. "I jam with a few guys down on Beale Street from time to time. Mostly I play for me."

She considered him thoughtfully, chewed the corner of her mouth and he had the uncomfortable sensation that she was peeking into his brain, accessing his most private thoughts. "You're very tactile, aren't you?"

"I suppose," Linc thought, though he'd never really thought about it before. He learned by touch—he could take things apart and put them back together much easier than he could understand an instruction manual. It was a trait that drove his family nuts. Cade, in particular. Linc had always been better at working on that yellow Corvette his brother adored than he had.

"So tell me about True Blue Bonds," she finally suggested. "Maybe I can help."

He grimaced, leaned back in his chair and passed a hand over his face. "I don't know what you think you can do."

She merely shrugged. "I might surprise you. I'm pretty resourceful."

He supposed she'd have to be in her line of work. Fine, he thought. He'd give it a shot. At this point, what did he have to lose? He outlined the problem, then tossed his napkin onto the table and waited while she mulled things over.

"So if profits are down, then your advertising budget is down with it, right?"

Directly to the heart of the matter. "Bingo."

"It's simple. You need to align yourself with someone else who is currently advertising. Someone *not* in the bail-bonds business, otherwise…"

"Otherwise it defeats the purpose," he finished. It was an excellent idea, but there was only one fly in the ointment. A droll smile rolled around his lips. "And who is it exactly that's going to want to split advertising fees with me?"

"Who do you help?"

"The local justice system."

"Then you should start there."

Linc chuckled. "The department of corrections isn't exactly running a big campaign right now."

"No, but your city council members are."

"You want me to hook up with a politician?" he asked skeptically. Wouldn't that do more harm than good? Didn't people hate politicians? Linc could honestly say that he voted and kept abreast of current politics, but more out of respect for the founding fathers and men and women who'd given their lives for his freedom and his right to vote than out of real interest.

"Who's running on a 'clean up the streets' platform?"

Linc mulled it over. There were several who were touting increased pay for civil servants, a larger police force and safer streets, but if he had to choose one as a front-runner on the issues, it would be Cecil Meeks. Furthermore, he was the incumbent. He shared his opinion with her. "That's who I'd say, anyway."

Georgia nodded succinctly. "Then that's who you need to talk to. From a marketing standpoint, he'd be a fool to refuse. Your company has an excellent reputation. You and your brother are both handsome." She pulled a shrug. "It's a win-win situation."

"You think I'm handsome?" he asked, secretly pleased and hit with the pressing urge to needle her.

Georgia blushed. "To the right type of woman, I am sure that you are irresistible."

Intrigued, Linc poked his tongue in his cheek and his amused gaze tangled with hers. "The right type of woman, eh? What, precisely, would that type be?" he drawled. Why was he asking this? he wondered. He had no desire whatsoever to be psychoanalyzed by a woman who had a disturbing penchant for being right.

"Pampers."

"As in diapers?" he asked, not following.

Georgia's milk chocolate gaze glittered with mirth. "The *disposable* kind."

Linc grimaced, shoved a hand through his hair. "Ouch."

"Oh, I doubt you're the one getting hurt," she said, chuckling knowingly.

Uncomfortable with the direction this conversation was going, Linc steered the dialogue back to the issue at hand. "So you really think I should try to talk Cecil Meeks into sharing some advertising with us?"

Georgia's gaze turned speculative and she finally nodded. "I think you could get him to do it for free," she said matter-of-factly. "A ringing endorsement from a couple of good-looking hometown heroes would go a long way toward sharpening his image."

Though he didn't relish the idea of aligning himself with a politician, he had to admit her idea was ingenious. Furthermore, he instinctively knew his father would like it. Cade, he imagined, would not, but since Linc had been the unlucky bastard who'd been saddled with the job of turning things around, he'd have no choice but to go along with it or come up with an alternative.

"Thanks, Georgia," he finally said. "I think you might be on to something."

She smiled, somewhat embarrassed. "You're welcome." She let go of a small breath. "So…what's on schedule for tomorrow?"

"More of the same, I'm afraid." He felt a grin tug at his lips. "Not nearly as exciting as *Dog,* eh?"

She heaved a dramatic sigh and propped her chin in the palm of her hand. "Well, I was hoping I'd at least get to use my stun gun."

A bark of laughter erupted from his throat. "You're kidding, right?"

She shot him a smile he found curiously endearing. "Have you forgotten that I bathe naked outside?"

Linc swallowed as that image materialized all too readily once again in his mind's eye. He felt his palms itch and a blanket of heat drape his loins. "So I've learned." He shot her an uncertain glance. "So you really have a stun gun?"

"I really do. My brother thought I needed the protection when I moved into my new house. I didn't like the idea of having a real gun, so I got the stun gun instead."

"Have you ever hit anyone with it?"

"Nope." Her smile capsized. "But I'd like to break it in on Carter," she said darkly.

Linc grinned. "I wouldn't mind seeing that."

"Don't worry," she assured him. "You will."

Since he'd entertained the idea of beating the hell out of the guy, he could hardly chide her for wanting to hit him with her stun gun.

"What?" she asked, darting him a look. "Aren't you going to tell me that I shouldn't do it? That I only *think* it'll make me feel better? That it's petty and beneath me?"

Linc took a pull from his beer. "Hell, no. Why would I do that?"

A slow smile curled her lips, then she grimaced adorably. "I figured somebody ought to try and talk me out of it."

"You aren't going to get any objections from me. After what he's put you through, I think he deserves that and more. Shock the shit out of him, sweetheart," Linc told her, chuckling softly. "What goes around comes around. I imagine you aren't the only person who wishes they could hit Carter Watkins with five-hundred volts."

Her gaze tangled with his again and another small smile curled those lush lips. "Try seven-seventy-five."

Linc whistled low and grinned at her. "I, uh… I guess a million was overkill."

She smiled and held her index finger barely above her thumb. "Just a little."

Though it was none of his business and he had no real reason—other than morbid curiosity—Linc asked the one question which had been driving him nuts from the get-go. "How in the hell did you get mixed up with someone like Carter Watkins?"

She quirked a brow. "You mean aside from sheer stupidity and poor judgment? I told you. We met at Marcello's."

"Yes, I knew that part. But what I want to know is *how?* Did he accidentally on purpose spill coffee on your shirt? Did he accidentally on purpose bump into you? Did he quote a line of poetry?" He glanced at her hair. *Did he tell you that ghastly ponytail was sexy?* Linc wondered silently, making himself chuckle.

Georgia frowned, evidently wanting in on the joke, but Linc knew better than to give voice to that uncharitable thought. Besides, he didn't know her well enough to tell her how to wear her hair. Yet, at any rate. And who was to say if the opportunity presented itself that he wouldn't encourage her to cease and desist with the onion-head do, anyway?

Evidently he'd stared at her hair too long, because she suddenly reached up and smoothed it, then uttered a startled little gasp. "Why didn't you tell me my hair was falling down?"

"Because I like it better that way." So much for waiting to know her better, being tactful, etc… But how could he resist an opening like that?

A stunned laugh burst from her throat and her eyes widened. "Oh," she said. "Well, thank you. I think."

"It was a compliment. The curls are nice." Mild understatement. He loved her curls, kept resisting the urge to wrap his fingers around one pretty strand and tug her closer for a kiss, where he could plunder that ripe mouth and suck on her bottom lip. "You've got pretty hair." He frowned and shook his head. "But that ponytail is ghastly."

Rather than being insulted, Georgia merely laughed. "Ghastly? Are they putting vocabulary words on the back of the Fruity Flakes box again?"

"I read," Linc told her, feigning insult.

"And I wear my hair like this for a reason, Mr. Helpful."

He winced. "Yes, but you don't need a facelift yet."

She inhaled sharply, then chuckled with outrage. "Jerk," she muttered.

Okay, he'd bite. "Why do you wear your hair like that?"

She chewed her bottom lip. "Did it ever occur to you that I happen to like it?"

"If you liked it you would have said so. That's not what you said," he pointed out. "You said you wore your hair like that for a reason. What's the reason?"

She paused to consider him and he got the curious feeling that he'd picked up on something she didn't intend to let slip. "There are two reasons actually," she finally confessed. "Number one, it's efficient. It takes me less than thirty seconds to put it up."

Linc nodded thoughtfully. "I can see where that would be important to you. What's reason number two?"

She took a sip of her tea. "You're going to think it's ridiculous."

"Since when do you care what I think?"

"Since when do you care how I wear my hair?" she shot back with a pointed look.

"I was only offering a little constructive criticism," Linc said, purposely goading her. He didn't know why. He just couldn't seem to help himself. For reasons he knew better than to explore, this was the most fun he'd had in a long time.

She bared her teeth in a smile. "Then I'm sure you won't mind when I reciprocate the gesture."

"Of course not. What's reason number two?"

"My brides."

Linc blinked. "Come again?"

"My brides," she repeated exasperatedly. "I need to look professional, not pretty. I don't want to be perceived as competition on any level to them. It's their wedding. It's their special day. Everyone else can look nice, but the bride is supposed to shine. She's the crown jewel of the ceremony."

Astounded, Linc felt his jaw drop. He'd heard of dumbing down before, but ugly-ing down? She'd lost her mind. He leaned forward. "You mean you wear your hair in that scalp-stretching, miserable-ass ponytail so that your brides can think they are prettier than you are?" he demanded, his voice escalating with outrage.

"In a manner of speaking."

Linc sighed, unreasonably annoyed over her tactic, and shook his head. "You're right. I do think it's ridiculous. And absurd and silly and just plain dumb." He glanced at her hair and muttered a curse. "You should wear it however you want to and the hell with the rest of them," he told her.

Georgia simply smiled. "I'll get my turn to be the crown jewel someday," she said. "Until then I don't mind being a lesser accessory."

No doubt she had her wedding all planned out, Linc thought, suddenly disturbed with the direction their conversation had taken. Right down to the last place card and petit four.

The mere idea made his head hurt, made his guts twist into a rope of dread around his middle. He mentally redressed her in the gown he'd seen in her window this morning, her hair down, her lips a promise of heaven hidden behind a veil, and a faceless man at her side who'd get to kiss those lips and take naked baths with her outside and

Shit.

"We should go," he said, abruptly rising from his chair. He tossed enough money on the table to cover the bill and impatiently waited for her to collect her things. All this talk of brides and weddings and crown jewels was making him break into a rash. His entire body itched.

"I should pick up the tab," she said, going into her purse for her wallet.

"You caught lunch. Let's go."

Looking bewildered, but resigned, Georgia followed him out to the truck. He drove her back over to her shop where the gown seemed to glow with an otherworldly luminescence and he couldn't look at it without imagining her in it.

"I'll pick you up at home in the morning," Linc told her.

He sure as hell wasn't coming back here.

Ever.

7

"So you're not coming to the office at all today?"

Cordless phone tucked between her shoulder and ear, Georgia stuffed her feet into her shoes and made sure that she turned the light off before heading downstairs. They'd already established that Linc was punctual, so she could count on him to be on time this morning. To make up for the prune Danish incident yesterday, she'd made a small breakfast. Nothing fancy, just the usual she tried to pull together for her and Jack a few times a week.

"No, I'm not," she confirmed. She made her way into the kitchen and pulled the biscuits she'd whipped up out of the oven. "He's picking me up here."

Karen hummed into the phone. "Why am I not surprised? He wins the Platinum-Diamond-Encrusted-Special-Snowflake Commitment-Phobic Award, hands down, in my opinion," she said, laughing. "I don't think a group of special-op Rangers could get your bounty hunter back in here at gunpoint, much less of his own volition."

Georgia chuckled under her breath. No doubt Karen was right about that. The instant the conversation had turned to weddings last night, Linc had become brooding, distant and impatient. Though she knew it was none of her business, she desperately wanted to know why he had such a serious aversion to the idea of sharing the rest of his life with one person.

When she'd made the offer to plan Gracie's wedding for free, she'd assumed that he'd accepted simply to make his sister happy and to make their lives easier. That was true, she knew, but Georgia suspected there was more to it than that. *What* exactly remained to be seen, but she had the irrepressible urge to find out. Poking around in Linc's business—or more accurately, his brain—was probably not the brightest move for a girl to make, but she'd taken bigger risks before. Hell, in her line of work she was always at odds with someone. Her lips quirked. Generally the mother of the bride.

"So how did it go yesterday?" Karen wanted to know "I tried to call you last night, but didn't get you."

That's because she'd been in her outside bath and had forgotten to bring the cordless handset with her.

Relaxing in the tub was her at-home stress therapy and after not finding Carter, not to mention spending the day in close proximity with Linc, her nerves had been shot. Quite frankly, she wasn't exactly sure which one had created more tension. Actually, that wasn't true—being with Linc created a tension of a different sort.

That of the nagging, inappropriate, sexual variety.

But honestly, how was she supposed to spend the better part of her day with him and *not* be affected? That haunting scent of patchouli combined with those sexy, heavy-lidded mossy eyes and that smile…

Georgia released a small breath.

That smile, just the simple act of rearranging his already sumptuous mouth into the universal symbol for happiness, made something in her chest warm and lurch, and made her nipples tingle with an *oh-mercy* kind of need.

Her gaze slid to the bowl on her table, the one that he'd made with those beautiful, strong hands. Her breath left her in a little whoosh as she imagined those hands working the clay, shaping it and molding it. It wasn't too much of a stretch to imagine those same hands sliding over her body, molding *her,* shaping *her,* bringing out the best in her.

Just being close to him made her go into a little

simmer of sensual longing the likes of which she'd
never experienced. When she'd landed against him
in the truck, Georgia had been more shaken by the
feel of that rock-hard body next to hers than being
unceremoniously slung across the cab. It was the
more, Georgia realized. And if she wasn't careful,
that *more* would be her undoing.

This, she concluded, given the circumstances—or
under any circumstances, for that matter—was *bad.*

In the first place, she should be worrying more
about finding Carter Watkins and her ring than con-
templating the lean slope of Linc's cheek, and the
corresponding heavy ache in her sex it seemed to
evoke. She shouldn't be stealing glances at his
profile and wondering if the masculine yet vulnerable side of his neck tasted as good as it looked.
She shouldn't be staring at his hands—strong, well-
shaped and capable—and imagining them sliding
over the small of her back, or pushing into her hair
as he pulled her closer for a kiss.

In short, she didn't have time and shouldn't be
lusting after a man who clearly had no interest in
forming any sort of lasting attachment. It was coun-
terproductive, the epitome of inefficiency.

And yet…she wanted him. Craved him. Needed
him.

"Did you get any leads on Carter?" Karen asked.

She sighed. "Not yet."

"I'm sorry, Georgia," her assistant told her. "I know this is hard."

The hardest part was knowing this was her fault, that it all could have been avoided if she'd only used better sense. Georgia swallowed. "Well, all I can do is keep looking."

"Does the badass know what he's doing?"

Georgia felt a smile slide over her lips. "Badass?"

Karen's chuckle drifted over the line. "Oh, you know he's a badass," she said. "And he's very good-looking. Funny how you forgot to mention that part."

"I didn't think it was relevant," Georgia lied. She just hadn't wanted Karen reading more into the situation than what was there. Or discovering the pitiful truth, that Linc Stone had the rare ability to turn both her brain and her body to mush.

"For future reference, any time you are going to be working with a hot man, it's *relevant.*"

"Hot, lukewarm or cold, it doesn't matter to me so long as he gets the job done."

"I can't speak for all men, but he can usually do it better when he's warmed up," Linc said from the screen door, startling the life out of her. She inhaled sharply and jumped.

"Ooo. Was that him?" Karen asked. "Is he there?"

When no hole immediately opened up in the floor for her to fall through, mortified and cheeks blazing, Georgia slowly turned around. Linc stood on her back step, his face wreathed in a wicked smile that made her belly tip in a warm roll. Dressed in a pair of well-worn jeans and a black cable-knit sweater, his hair still a little wet from his shower, her badass bounty hunter looked better than good-looking—he was *lethal.*

"Er…yes," Georgia finally replied, as Karen kept repeating the question in her ear. "I'll check in with you later." She disconnected and motioned for Linc to come inside.

"You're awfully cocky this morning," Georgia quipped, setting the phone back onto its base.

"So you *were* talking about me," Linc said, evidently pleased. He absently scratched his chest. "I knew you thought I was handsome, but didn't know I'd been bumped up to hot."

"Karen thinks you're hot," Georgia clarified. "I think you're a pain in the ass."

He sidled over to the stove and spied the country ham and biscuits she'd made this morning. "If I'm such a pain in the ass, why did you make me breakfast?"

"Because I can't trust you in public. In light of the Danish-tossing incident yesterday morning, I thought I should err on the side of caution." She paused. "Besides, it's not all for you. My brother will be by in a minute." She gestured to the bag on the counter. "He'll take his to go."

Linc paused. "Since he doesn't know about the ring, who am I supposed to be and why the hell am I here so early?"

Oh, shit, Georgia thought, a dart of unease lodging in her chest. She didn't have to worry about Jack knowing Linc—they didn't exactly move in the same circles. But she hadn't thought that far ahead. She opened her mouth, hoping to form some sort of excuse, but heard the alarm sound at the end of the driveway, indicating that her time was limited. Dammit, why hadn't she heard it when Linc pulled through? It would have saved her a hell of a lot of embarrassment. No, she'd been too busy letting Karen yak away in her ear to hear him. Bloody hell.

"Don't worry," Linc assured her. He lifted his brows and smiled one of those significant smiles that made her distinctly nervous. "I'll improvise. You follow my lead, remember?"

"That won't be necessary. I—" She heard her brother's truck door slam. "Don't embarrass me," Georgia said through gritted teeth, shooting him a death-ray glare. "My brother has never—"

Jack rapped a couple of times on the door, then

pulled it open. "Morning, sis," he said, then drew up short as his gaze landed on Linc.

And no wonder.

He'd never seen a man at her house before. Through no accident, he'd been out of town the one night she'd let Carter come over. She didn't pry into Jack's relationships and didn't want him to pry into hers. Furthermore, she was his little sister and he was quite protective. If anyone ought to understand that, Linc should.

Linc immediately stuck out his hand. "Linc Stone. You must be Jack. Georgia's told me a lot about you."

Her brother's gaze slid to her as he shook Linc's proffered hand. "That must be nice. I've never heard of you."

Georgia laughed nervously as the testosterone level in the room spiked to unhealthy proportions. "Haven't had the time," she said. "Working late, you know."

"I just talked to you last night," Jack pointed out, his voice a guarded growl. "You didn't mention you'd be having overnight company."

In the first place, she hadn't had overnight company, and in the second place, if she had it was none of his damned business. "I—"

Linc frowned at her, his gaze becoming increasingly irritated. "You didn't mention it to me, either. Who spent the night with you, baby?"

Baby? What the hell— "Nobody spent the night with me," Georgia said, exasperated. She glared at Jack. "Linc's my—"

Linc slung an arm around her shoulder, pulled her close, inadvertently setting off a heat bomb in her belly. Her nipples sizzled and the side of her body currently snugged against his felt like it had been slapped against a furnace. "—boyfriend," he finished for her, and it was a damned good thing that he'd put an arm around her, otherwise she would have fallen over in shock. "I'm her boyfriend. It's a pleasure to meet you." He smiled, though there was a distinctly proprietary gleam in his gaze which made her silly heart do a little pirouette, despite the fact she knew it was fake. This was the classic pissing contest between two alpha males and unfortunately, she was stuck right in the middle.

And no doubt she'd be the one getting pissed on.

Jack stared at her for a minute, clearly torn between removing Linc's arm from her body and minding his own business. Thankfully years of her not interfering in his personal affairs paid off.

"Nice to meet you," he finally told Linc, albeit gruffly and grudgingly. He picked up his bag from the counter along with his thermal coffee cup and shot her a look. "I'd better get going. I'll call you later."

And you'd better be ready to explain hung unspoken in the air.

Once she'd heard Jack's engine start once more, she slipped out from beneath Linc's arm and glared up at him. "Boyfriend?" she asked shrilly, her voice vibrating with an emotion she didn't recognize. *"Boyfriend?* Have you lost your mind?"

"YES," LINC REPLIED. "But not my appetite." Still trying to figure out what the hell had possessed him to make such a moronic statement to her brother, Linc settled himself at her kitchen table and helped himself to a slice of ham and a biscuit. "I don't suppose I could talk you into making some redeye gravy, could I?"

"I'm more tempted to bean you over the head with the frying pan," Georgia told him. "I can't believe you just did that."

"Come on," he cajoled. "You know how to make it, don't you?"

Looking adorably annoyed, she harrumphed under her breath. "Of course I know how to make it. It's ham drippings and coffee, for pity's sake." She rolled her eyes. "It's not baked Alaska."

Georgia poured him a cup of coffee and unceremoniously thunked it down next to his plate, then opened the refrigerator and pulled out a jar of homemade strawberry preserves and set it on the table, as well. "Here," she said. "You might as well try this while you wait."

Linc felt a smile twitch on his lips. She was more a grudging hostess than grateful, but he'd take it. He was used to getting a home-cooked dinner thanks to Cade, but breakfast was a rare treat. "Thanks," he murmured. "So I take it your brother isn't used to seeing men around here?"

He knew the answer, of course. The equally thunderous and shocked expression on Jack Hart's face had been evidence enough. Though he knew she'd made the mistake with Carter, Linc had to admit something about knowing that she was ordinarily quite selective with her male company made him inordinately happy. Which was ignorant when he wasn't supposed to care. Still…

He heard Georgia sigh. "No, he isn't." She poured a bit of coffee into the pan and a gratifying sizzle met Linc's ears. "In fact, that's the first time it's ever happened."

Linc slipped a little bite of ham to Stitch, who'd come to beg at his chair. "Didn't you tell me that Carter took the ring from your house?"

"I did."

The Harlequin Reader Service® — Here's how it works:

Accepting your 2 free books and 2 free gifts places you under no obligation to buy anything. You may keep the books and gifts and return the shipping statement marked "cancel". If you do not cancel, about a month later we'll send you 6 additional books and bill you just $3.99 each in the U.S. or $4.47 each in Canada, plus 25¢ shipping & handling per book and applicable taxes if any.* That's the complete price and — compared to cover prices of $4.75 each in the U.S. and $5.75 each in Canada — it's quite a bargain! You may cancel at any time, but if you choose to continue, every month we'll send you 6 more books which you may either purchase at the discount price or return to us and cancel your subscription.

*Terms and prices subject to change without notice. Sales tax applicable in N.Y. Canadian residents will be charged applicable provincial taxes and GST. Credit or debit balances in a customer's account(s) may be offset by any other outstanding balance owed by or to the customer. Please allow 4 to 6 weeks for delivery. Offer available while quantities last.

If offer card is missing write to: Harlequin Reader Service, 3010 Walden Ave., P.O. Box 1867, Buffalo NY 14240-1867

NO POSTAGE
NECESSARY
IF MAILED
IN THE
UNITED STATES

BUSINESS REPLY MAIL
FIRST-CLASS MAIL   PERMIT NO. 717   BUFFALO, NY

POSTAGE WILL BE PAID BY ADDRESSEE

**HARLEQUIN READER SERVICE
3010 WALDEN AVE
PO BOX 1867
BUFFALO NY 14240-9952**

Play the Lucky Hearts Game

and get...

2 FREE BOOKS and
2 FREE MYSTERY GIFTS...
YOURS to KEEP!

yes! I have scratched off the silver card. Please send me my *2 FREE BOOKS* and *2 FREE mystery GIFTS.* I understand that I am under no obligation to purchase any books as explained on the back of this card.

Scratch Here!
then look below to see what your cards get you... 2 Free Books & 2 Free Mystery Gifts!

351 HDL ENSW   151 HDL ENZW

FIRST NAME

LAST NAME

ADDRESS

APT.#

CITY

STATE/PROV.

ZIP/POSTAL CODE

(H-B-11/07)

Twenty-one gets you
2 FREE BOOKS and
2 FREE MYSTERY GIFTS!

Twenty gets you
2 FREE BOOKS!

Nineteen gets you
1 FREE BOOK!

TRY AGAIN!

Offer limited to one per household and not valid to current Harlequin® Blaze® subscribers. All orders subject to approval.
Your Privacy – Harlequin Books is committed to protecting your privacy. Our Privacy Policy is available online at www.eHarlequin.com or upon request from the Harlequin Reader Service. From time to time we make our lists of customers available to reputable firms who may have a product or service of interest to you. If you would prefer for us not to share your name and address, please check here. ☐

▲ DETACH AND MAIL CARD TODAY! ▲

© 2002 HARLEQUIN ENTERPRISES LTD.
® and ™ are trademarks owned and used by the trademark owner and/or its licensee.

"But Jack never met him?" Now that was interesting. She'd dated the guy for a month and had never introduced him to her brother? Why not? Linc wondered, the plot thickening.

Georgia poured the gravy into a little ceramic boat and brought it to the table. "No. Carter was only here the one time and Jack was out of town on business."

No doubt that was on purpose, Linc thought, judging from her brother's reaction this morning. "Is he ordinarily so protective?"

Her lips quirked with wry humor. "What do you think? I still can't believe you told him you were my boyfriend. What the hell were you thinking?"

He poured gravy over his ham. "I was thinking that I couldn't tell him the real reason I was here, and the boyfriend angle seemed like the best scenario."

At least, that was the logical reason. The illogical reason had something to do with marking his territory and not caring for the way her brother had looked at him, as though he were suspicious parasite hanging around his sister. Linc knew that look—the few times his own sister had brought home a new guy, he'd worn the same don't-fuck-with-her expression.

Curiously, Linc didn't like being on the receiving end of that look. It had annoyed and goaded him into an action he ordinarily wouldn't have taken, particularly with Georgia, or Trouble as he'd decided to call her. He speared another bite of his breakfast and shot her a brooding look.

Hair down this morning as opposed to the infernal ponytail and dressed in another pair of jeans, Roper boots and a burnt orange sweater, Georgia carefully slathered butter and jam on her biscuit. The bright morning sun poured through windows, painting copperish highlights in her dark brown curly hair and a rosy glow bloomed on her cheeks. Despite being irritated with him, she looked relaxed and content, fresh-scrubbed and invigorated.

A thought struck. "Have you been out this morning?"

She looked up, a frown creasing her brow. "Out where?"

"Outside. Have you been riding?"

She nodded. "I try to ride every morning, why?"

Linc felt a smile tug at the corner of his mouth. "I can tell."

"How?"

"You're not as uptight."

A droll grin shaped her lips as she finished chewing a bite of her biscuit. "Thanks. I think." She swallowed thoughtfully. "And thank you for not telling my brother the real reason you're here. Not that I liked how you improvised, but…" She pulled a helpless shrug. "I suppose it's better than the alternative."

"It'll actually work to our advantage," Linc told her. "I'm going to be in and out of here until we find Carter, so we need to have some sort of game plan in place."

Finished eating, she stood and started clearing the table. "Yeah, well. Remember this. When the time comes for us to break up, I'm ditching you, hoss, not the other way around."

A bark of laughter erupted from Linc's throat. "Why do you get to dump me?"

"Because I called it."

Smiling, he followed her to the sink and rinsed his cup. "You called it?" he asked. "What are we? Four?"

"Hey, you're the one who made up this fake relationship." She smiled and leaned a hip against the counter. "It's only fair that I get to be the one who calls it quits."

Linc considered her for a moment. "What reason are you going to give for cutting me loose?"

"Oh," Georgia said, chuckling knowingly. "Don't worry. It'll be something good."

That certainly sounded ominous, Linc thought, staring at her. At that lush, ripe mouth specifically.

God help him, he wanted to taste her. *Needed* to taste her. "When you say good, just what exactly do you mean?"

Georgia paused to look at him, those chocolate eyes crinkled at the corners. "Well, it goes without saying that I'll have to have a good reason for dumping you. And my good reason will have to coincide with some sort of bad behavior on your part." She chewed the corner of her lip consideringly. "Tell you what. I'm a reasonable woman. I'll give you a choice. You can either be a cheating bastard or a premature ejaculator. Take your pick."

A sharp chuckle burst from his throat. Dishonest or emasculated? He should have known. "What's behind door number three?"

"I caught you wearing my panties," she said without missing a beat.

Linc laughed again. "How about I get back to you on that?"

Georgia smiled, though a flash of seriousness lit her gaze. "Of course, I could always tell the truth."

"And what would that be?" He knew the minute the words left his mouth he shouldn't have asked the question.

"That you're commitment-phobic to the *nth* degree and that keeping you around simply because you're handsome and charming, and no doubt a great kisser and hot in the sack, would be an exercise in heartbreak and futility."

Linc stilled and his gaze tangled with hers. If wanting to stay single and commitment-phobic were synonymous then she'd hit the nail on the head.

It was the rest of what she said that he found infinitely more intriguing.

"Sounds like you've given this a lot of thought."

"Nah," Georgia said, evidently realizing she'd said too much. He watched her pulse flutter wildly in her throat and she nervously played with a hand towel, avoiding his gaze.

Smiling, Linc sidled closer to her. "You think I'm handsome?"

With a long-suffering sigh, she glanced at him once more. "We've already established that. I told you last night that you were handsome. It's not a state secret, for heaven's sake." She rolled her eyes. "You own a mirror."

Odd how he'd never realized how sexy a provoking female could be. "You think I'm charming?"

"In your own boorish way, yes," she admitted.

"What makes you think I'm a great kisser and—" he pretended to be searching his memory for the correct phrase though naturally his ego hadn't let him forget it "—hot in the sack, I believe is what you said?"

"Intuition," Georgia said, a bit breathlessly. "But I don't require any p-proof."

But she wanted it, Linc realized, recognizing his own desire in hers. *Pupils dilated, shallow breaths, her gaze lingering on his mouth...* Oh, yeah. She definitely wanted it.

"Are you sure?" he asked softly, cupping her jaw. Unable to resist, he slipped the pad of his thumb across her bottom lip and had the pleasure of watching her eyes go all sleepy and melting. Her sweet breath washed over his hand, making his belly quake. "Since I'm your boyfriend and all," he whispered. He lowered his head, put his mouth a hairbreadth from hers, drawing out the tension, making her lean forward.

"But you're not really my boy—"

"Shh," Linc told her. "Follow my lead, remember?"

Then, because he'd clearly lost his mind and any semblance of self-control, he fitted his lips over hers. They were plump and pillowy-soft, sweetened with strawberry jam and butter, and the first taste of her against his tongue rattled the cage around his heart with enough force to shatter the lock. An unrecognizable emotion whipped through him, tearing him up from the inside out.

Holy mother of—

A little sigh of supplication eddied out of her mouth and into his, and that one tiny breath was all it took for Linc to push his hands deeper into those beautiful curls he'd been fantasizing about for the past few days. His dick jerked hard against his zipper and he shifted, trying desperately not to let the damned thing leap right out of the top of his jeans. Fire licked through his veins and his balls hardened to the point just shy of pain.

A little mewl of pleasure issued from Georgia's throat as she went up on tiptoe and twined her arms around his neck. Her sweet tongue tangled around his, exploring his mouth with a fervor that was at once seductive and wondrous, as though she'd received some sort of confirmation, had found something she'd been looking for but had always hovered just out of reach.

God help him, Linc thought…because Trouble tasted good. In fact, he could easily see himself becoming addicted to it.

8

SO SHE'D BEEN RIGHT, Georgia thought as Linc's hard body molded perfectly against hers.

This was the *more*.

This coming apart at the seams, burning inferno of desire ripping through her body, making every hair on her being stand on end, her nipples pearl and her sex weep was the *it* she'd been missing.

The tiny, miniscule part of her brain that recognized that this was a bad idea knew that she should pull away, that she should stop "following his lead" as it were. But the rest of her brain—the part that was consumed with indulging her inner sexually under-privileged bad girl—wouldn't let her. Instead, she wrapped her arms around his neck and pressed herself shamelessly against him. He tasted like strong coffee and salty ham, like wickedness and sin…heavenly, Georgia thought dimly.

Linc groaned into her mouth, rasped his tongue against hers in the most toe-curling fashion. In and out, in and out, an erotic waltz of taste and sensation. The faint scent of patchouli and soap teased her nostrils and those big warm hands gently cupped her face and pushed into her hair, kneading her scalp. She felt her muscles go all weak, her belly muddle with heat. Tactile, she thought dimly, wondering if she'd become like clay in his hands, as well. It was so damned wonderful it made her bones melt, made her want to scale his body and dissolve all over him. An insistent throb built between her legs, pounding with every beat of her heart, making her squirm even closer to him, an itch that begged to be scratched.

And if he was this good at kissing, then…mercy.

Without warning, Linc lifted her off the floor and set her on top of the counter. His lips never leaving hers, he sidled into the open vee between her legs, putting himself in the optimal itch-scratching position. The first hint of pressure against her aching clit ripped the breath from her lungs and she felt him smile against her lips. She could taste what that smile meant—male satisfaction, victory—and savored it by pulling him even closer to her. He was hard to her soft, eager to her willing, and heaven help her, if he so much as crooked his finger at this moment, she'd follow his lead anywhere.

He rocked against her once more, left off her mouth and nibbled and breathed into her ear, causing a wave of gooseflesh to wash over her. "Damn, you taste good," Linc whispered, his voice deep and sexy.

Georgia turned and licked a path over his neck, as well, and she had the pleasure of feeling his arms quake around her. The very idea that she could make this big, strong man quiver from a simple touch was intoxicating. "You taste like I was right."

Linc chuckled and drew back to look at her. "What do you mean?"

"You taste like a good kisser."

"Yeah, well, keep kissing me and I'll taste like I'm hot in the sack, too."

That's what she was afraid of, Georgia thought, resting her forehead against his. Kissing Linc was one thing—sleeping with him was another altogether. Though she wanted to. Heaven help her how she wanted to. She wanted to feel those hands slipping over her naked skin, his hot mouth attached to her breast, sucking her, eating her. She wanted to feel him lodged deeply between her thighs, filling her up, taking her until every ounce of energy was rung from her body.

She just…wanted.

He was wrong, she decided. She didn't have to "taste" him anymore to prove her hot-in-the-sack theory.

She knew it.

Luckily, Stitch decided he needed to go out before she could do anything stupid—like drag Linc upstairs—and telegraphed this message by hauling one of his diapers into the kitchen.

Linc looked down at the dog and chuckled. "Why doesn't he just bark at the door?"

Georgia felt a small smile move over her lips. "Too passé." She sighed. "I'd better take him out," she said, glad for the excuse.

When she returned, Linc was on the phone. "Cecil Meeks," he mouthed to her. "I'm glad to hear it, Cecil," Linc was saying. "I think it would be a good PR move for both of us. Right," he said. "Right. Okay, I'll line up Cade and we'll meet you there at ten. Sure. No, that's no problem. The sooner we get the ads out the better off we are. All right," he said. "We'll see you there." He disconnected, looked at Georgia and winced regrettably. "Small change of plans. I need to do a quick detour today and have some pictures made with Cecil for the new ad campaign he wants to implement."

Georgia grinned, pleased that he'd thought her advice had merit. "You didn't waste any time contacting him, did you?"

Linc inclined his head. "I called him last night on my way home. You were right. He jumped on the idea. Said getting our support would be the boost that he needed. Evidently, Sunny Templeton is giving him a run for his money." He clipped his phone back into the holder at his waist. "You don't mind, do you?"

Actually, this would work to her advantage. "Not if you don't mind letting me take care of something today, as well."

"What is it?" he asked, looking endearingly grim. "We don't have to go to a wedding, do we?"

"No," she said, poking her tongue into her cheek. "I just need to pick up something for one of my brides." Point of fact, picking up this something was going to be embarrassing enough to start with, but taking care of that errand now, in light of what had just happened between them... Eek.

Linc nodded. "Fine. I don't suppose I can argue."

"Oh, you can," Georgia assured him, laughing. She grabbed her purse and held open the back door for him. "It's just a matter of whether you will or not."

"Smart-ass."

"What did your brother think about the advertising idea?"

Linc double-checked to make sure her door was locked. "I haven't exactly told him yet."

Georgia felt her eyes widen. "But didn't you just tell Cecil the two of you would meet him somewhere at ten?"

He opened the passenger door for her. "I did."

"Then how are you going to get Cade there? What if he's busy?"

"Then he'll just have to stop what he's doing."

Georgia climbed into the cab and fastened her seat belt as Linc rounded the hood. He slid behind the wheel. "Will he do that?"

"He won't like it, but he will."

Georgia shrugged, but didn't say anything else. What was the point? Who was she to try and point out that Linc's high-handedness might not be appreciated? Then again, Cade Stone was probably used to it. It would be fun to watch, in any case.

Linc backed up and aimed his SUV down her driveway. "So where's your errand? In Germantown?"

"Actually it's in Memphis," Georgia said. "If we'd known about your plans with Cecil I could have just met you this morning."

He grinned and shot her a look that made her palms tingle. "Then you would have missed out on tasting me to make sure I was a good kisser."

Georgia felt her cheeks pinken and she rolled her eyes. Like she was going to forget? Ha. Rather than respond, she directed the conversation back to practical matters—like organizing their day. "I'm assuming that you're meeting Cecil in Memphis, right?"

Linc nodded. "That's right."

She blew out a breath. "I know that I'm supposed

to be following your lead, but why don't we head on over to that part of town and get our errands out of the way before we come back to Germantown and start looking for Carter again?"

Linc smiled at her, those mossy green eyes twinkling with wicked humor. "You just can't help it, can you?"

Though she knew perfectly well what he was talking about, Georgia quirked a brow and played the innocent. "Help what?"

"Putting every duck in a row. Making sure there's no 'downtime.' Being in charge."

"Well, in this case time is of the essence, right? Every minute Carter is on the street is one more minute my mother's ring is at risk."

"We'll find him, Georgia," Linc told her, suddenly serious.

She couldn't help but notice that he didn't assure her they'd find the ring. Of course, if she'd learned one thing about Linc Stone over the past few days— aside from the fact that he could kiss her lips off and incinerate her good sense—she'd learned that he wasn't a liar. You might not like what he had to say, but he wasn't the type of guy to let a little thing like that keep him from telling the truth.

"Tell you what. Why don't we run this mysterious errand of yours first, then we'll head over to my place for a few minutes?" His expression darkened. "I need to bounty-hunter-up a little more for this picture with Cecil."

Georgia sent him a sidelong glance. "Bounty-hunter-up?"

"Cecil wants us decked out in black, in full-on catch-the-bad-guys mode. I need to change jeans."

"Won't you need to let Cade know?"

Linc grinned. "Cade's always in full bounty-hunter regalia."

Smiling, Georgia inclined her head. "Okay."

It sounded like a good plan to her. Very efficient. Furthermore, getting another peek into Linc's lair was intensely appealing. The last time she'd been too aware of him and his bare chest to properly take a look around. She'd seen enough to know that she'd misjudged his character, but what other secrets were there? Georgia wondered. If she looked close enough, what else would she discover? No doubt only things that would make him that much more appealing. She sighed.

And the last thing she needed was another reason to like Linc Stone. Lusting after him was bad enough.

"YOU'VE GOT TO BE kidding me," Linc said, staring through the plate-glass window of the store Georgia—Little Miss Friggin' Efficient—had directed him to. Linc read the sign emblazoned on the pink-and-green striped awning and inwardly shuddered with dread.

The Honeymoon, specializing in bridal lingerie since 1969.

Georgia merely chuckled. "You're welcome to wait in the car," she said, implying, of course, that she knew he thought his balls would shrivel up and fall off if he went inside. Talk about galling. A stabbing pain developed behind his right eye.

Linc released a sigh and passed a hand over his face. "Tell me again why we're here."

"We're here because I've had something special-ordered for one of my brides and I need to pick it up."

"What are you doing ordering lingerie for one of your brides? Why didn't her fiancé order it for her? Isn't that a bit creepy, Georgia? I mean, shouldn't your job end with the reception, or do these fools need your help with the honeymoon, too?"

Georgia arched a brow, a keen gleam entering her gaze. "Fools? What makes you think they're fools?"

Linc snorted. "They're getting married, aren't they?"

She studied him thoughtfully for a moment,

forcing him to resist the urge to squirm under that keen scrutiny. "Only fools get married?"

"Only fools fall in love—complete idiots get married."

Though she didn't so much as flinch, Linc could tell he'd just sent Georgia reeling. Her eyes widened with shock and a short burst of laughter erupted from her throat. Of course, he'd just insulted her profession, her beliefs, and every person—including her belated parents—who'd ever married.

After a moment, she cleared her throat. "Have you shared these feelings with your sister, by any chance?"

"Of course not," Linc told her, regretting his outburst. She'd be psychoanalyzing the hell out of him now, trying to poke around in his brain and see why wasn't interested in love and all it entailed. "But she knows that I never intend to fall in love and follow the natural progression down the aisle."

"So you think you can choose whether or not you fall in love? That it's a voluntary emotion?"

He thought it was time for this conversation to be over, that's what he thought. "I think I've managed to do it thus far." He climbed out of the truck, effectively changing the subject and leaving her no choice but to follow. "Come on. Let's get this over with."

"I told you that you could stay here," Georgia said.

"Yes, well, since you only *think* you're in charge, what you tell me is sort of moot, isn't it?"

"Why are you so pissy all of the sudden?" she snapped. "It's a lingerie store. It's not like we're here to have you neutered. Though it's damned tempting," she muttered under her breath as he held the door open for her.

"You're not big enough, Trouble," Linc said, chuckling despite himself.

She shot him a look over her shoulder. "Trouble?"

"Your new nickname. I thought you would prefer it to pain in the ass."

"I actually prefer Georgia," she said, her voice an irritated combination of evil and sweet. "But since you've given me a nickname, I'll be sure to come up with one for you."

"Knock yourself out, babe," he said, pulling a shrug. "I don't mind."

"Good. How does dickwad suit you?"

Linc strangled on a laugh.

"Morning, Ava," Georgia called, hailing a clerk. "Betty said I could come by today and pick up the special order for Tina Scarpone."

Ava smiled. "If her mother finds out about this, she'll ruin you, you know that, don't you?"

Georgia waited at the counter and smiled. "That's why her mother isn't going to find out. Besides, it's not her mother's honeymoon—it's Tina's. And Tina doesn't want to wear twenty yards of ruffled cotton." She chuckled. "She wants to knock David's socks off, not smother him."

Intrigued, despite the fact that he was surrounded by oodles of miserably-ever-after white lingerie— most of it tame by his standards—Linc sidled closer to where Georgia stood. He arrived just in time to watch Ava lift the lid off a box, presumably the one they'd come to pick up.

Georgia oohed appropriately and lifted the sheer, naughty nightie out of the package. It was more gauze and ribbon than actual fabric. White satin ribbon was shot through the sheer material and criss-crossed over the abdomen, then tied directly below and between the equally sheer cups. A tiny berib-boned thong completed the outfit.

That was it.

Every ounce of moisture evaporated from his mouth, staring at the teeny white negligee. Frankly he'd always preferred black or red, but white had just moved to the top of his list.

This was what Georgia had picked out for her bride? This measly scrap of guaranteed sex? What? No frilly robe to go over it? No cover-up of any sort?

His gaze darted around the store, taking in all of the other froufrou outfits, but nothing even came close to the sinful little number she was currently putting back in the box.

My God, he thought, stunned. He should have been used to her shocking the hell out of him by now, but for whatever reason, this new development trumped every other curve she'd thrown at him over the past couple of days. Naturally, he would have expected her to order something prim and pretty with lots of lacy fabric.

The nightie she was currently deeming *perfect* was one of the most sinful things he'd ever laid eyes on. A flame of heat wound through his belly and settled in his loins, and his mouth watered, imagining her in it instead.

"That's beautiful," Georgia was saying, clearly pleased. "What do you think?" she asked Ava. "Thigh-highs or no?"

"Men love thigh-highs," Linc heard himself say, his voice curiously thick and strangled even to his own ears.

Georgia turned to him, a calculating gleam in her eye. "You know, you may end up being useful after all."

He frowned, trying to figure out the insult. "Useful after all?"

She grabbed his arm and steered him toward the

back of the store to a rack of shoes. "I mean, you can help me put this together."

Oh, hell no, Linc thought, backing up. "Forget it," he said flatly. "Haven't I already told you I thought this was creepy?"

"What's creepy is that Tina's mother wants her to wear the same gown she did on her own honeymoon. That's *creepy.*"

Linc sure as hell couldn't argue with that, but was still disinclined to offer an opinion. This was something that Tina and David should be doing together, or that Tina should be doing alone. Unless they were picking out something for her to wear for him, they needed to stay the hell out of it.

She picked up two pairs of shoes. "I'm not asking you to try them on, dammit. I just want you to tell me—from a male point of view," she emphasized, "which one's are sexier."

"Georgia, I—"

She kicked her boots off, removed her socks and slipped one of each of the shoes on her feet. "Which ones look better?"

She had surprisingly small feet, Linc noted, suddenly distracted from their argument, her toes painted in a pretty pink shade. He caught a glimpse of something on the top of her foot and felt a line emerge between his brows. "What's that?"

"What's what?"

"That," Linc said, bending down to slip the shoe off of her foot. "Well, I'll be damned," he breathed, looking at the small green frog tattoo sitting atop her dainty foot. A surprised grin curving his lips, he looked up at her and his impressed gaze met hers. "You've got a tattoo?"

"I do. Let me guess? I'm not staying in the box again?"

That was putting it lightly. One would think he would have learned by now not to be surprised by anything when it came to Georgia Hart, but clearly he hadn't learned his lesson. Linc grinned at her. "Why a frog?"

"It's the nickname my dad gave me. I always slept with my legs drawn up—like a frog," she explained.

Though he knew it was insane, he was suddenly hit with the almost uncontrollable urge to kiss her instep, then make his way up the inside of her leg. He'd have to remove her pants first, but he wouldn't let a little thing like clothes stand in the way of tasting her.

Furthermore, if she'd been hiding a tattoo all this time, what other things about her were yet to be discovered? What other treasures could she be concealing? What other surprises were still in store?

Still holding her foot, Linc traced the outline of

her tattoo with his fingertip. So soft, he thought. And so incredibly sexy.

"Linc?"

He looked up. "Yeah?"

She smiled down at him, those melting chocolate eyes distinctly sweet and sultry. "Which shoes?"

"Neither," Linc told her. "Barefoot is best. And forget the thigh-highs, too."

"But I thought you said men liked thigh-highs?"

"They do." He grinned at her. "But naked is always best."

"So you're saying I should forget the negligee, as well?"

"No. I like that."

Georgia chuckled. "It's not for you, remember?"

Oh, yeah. Shit. He was losing his damned mind. He cast a brooding look at Georgia, the current author of his insanity.

And it was all her fault.

If she was taking this much time and effort on one of her brides' honeymoon attire, then he could only imagine that the same energy or more would be invested in hers, Linc decided.

Once again a vision of Georgia in that gown in her store window materialized in his mind's eye— the infernal faceless groom at her side—bringing the panic and irritation it always did. His belly clenched, his palms began to sweat and an urgency and desperation he couldn't explain twisted his insides into a Celtic knot of dread.

It was the groom that was getting to him, Linc decided, stunned. The lucky bastard.

9

"I SHOULD KICK YOUR ASS for this," Cade Stone muttered from the corner of his smiling mouth to Linc. "And I'm not so sure that I won't."

"Don't blame me," Linc said. He jerked his head in Georgia's direction. "It was her idea."

Standing off to the side while Cade and Linc finished getting ready for their photo shoot with Cecil Meeks, Georgia just laughed. "Hey, don't pass the buck this way, buddy. It's not my fault you didn't clear this with him first."

Cade shot her a dark glance. "That's because he knew I would say no."

"No isn't an option," Linc replied. "Now flash those pearly whites so that we can get this over with."

The photographer who'd been testing the lighting grimaced. "There's no point in flashing anything until Mr. Meeks arrives. He should be here shortly."

Georgia settled into a nearby chair and watched

the Stone brothers bicker back and forth. Though you could definitely tell they were from the same gene pool, Cade seemed rougher around the edges. He was a bit taller—which was saying something because Linc was easily six and a half feet—a bit broader, and there was a guardedness about him that immediately tugged at her heartstrings. He'd known pain and, for whatever reason, she suspected Linc had known the same one, only it had affected him on a different level. Where this insight came from she had no idea, but she knew it all the same.

Interesting, Georgia thought, watching the two of them. It was quite clear that Cade was the protector of the family and that Linc instinctively understood that. He accepted his role and seemed grateful to Cade for the support. Having her own overprotective brother, this was a sentiment Georgia understood fully.

"Got any leads on Carter yet?" Cade asked Linc.

Linc grimaced and shook his head. "Not yet, but we're going to start pounding the pavement again as soon as we finish up here."

"You still think he's in town?"

Linc slid her a look—just to see how closely she was following the conversation, she imagined. "Yeah. That's what I'm hoping, at any rate. His usual haunts have turned up empty, but we haven't canvassed the hotels yet. Those are next on our agenda."

"Keep me posted. And let me know if you need any help bringing him in." The significant way he delivered the line told Georgia it was merely code speak for "let me help you kick his ass."

Linc grinned. "I don't think I'm going to need any help. Trouble over there is packing a stun gun."

Cade shot her a double take and his mouth hitched up in an impressed smile. "Trouble?"

"It's my nickname. Want to know what your brother's is?" she asked sweetly.

"Here's Cecil," Linc announced, looking relieved.

Cade considered her for a minute, his gaze every bit as keen and insightful as his brother's. "I'll get back to you on that."

"You stay the hell away from her. The last thing she needs is encouragement. Or more ammunition," he added darkly.

"Gentlemen," Cecil announced. "I see you're ready." While he launched into his good-old-boy spiel, Georgia took the opportunity to call and check in with Karen.

"Weddings With Hart, this is Karen."

"Morning," she said, leaning back against the chair. She picked at a loose seam on her pants. "What's going on?"

"You mean aside from the fact that your brother

called me this morning and wanted the lowdown on Linc Stone?"

A dart of panic landed in Georgia's chest and she instinctively leaned forward once again. "You didn't tell him anything, did you?"

"Of course not," Karen told her, seemingly exasperated that Georgia would even ask. "I merely corroborated what he'd already been told. I wish I would have known you were going to take the boyfriend angle, otherwise I wouldn't have bumbled around like a secretive ass with your brother."

"*I* didn't know we were going to take the boyfriend angle." Her gaze slid to Linc who was presently smiling for the camera. Even knowing it was fake didn't prevent it from packing a punch, Georgia thought. Mercy, that man was sex on two feet. "Suffice it to say there was too much testosterone in the room this morning and Linc decided to wing things." She sighed. "Ultimately, it's for the best. He's going to be around a good bit until we find Carter and I don't need Jack asking questions." That was mild understatement. Though she knew he would love her no matter what, she couldn't bear the thought of having to tell him what she'd done—that she'd lost their mother's ring.

"He said Linc made him nervous."

Georgia grinned. "That's because they're too

much alike. One heartbreaker would recognize another, wouldn't you think?"

"Yeah, well, your heartbreaker brother has asked me to regularly update him on your status with Linc."

"He wants my own help to spy on me for him?" she asked, outraged. "He'd throttle me if I ever tried anything like that with him."

Karen chuckled. "That occurred to me, as well. Don't worry. I'll just feed him false reports. This will actually work to both our advantages."

Oh, Lord. She knew where this was going. "What do you mean?"

"Well, I can tell him whatever you want me to tell him, and it gives me the opportunity to get to know him better. Win-win. See?" she asked brightly.

"Karen," Georgia said, pouring every ounce of caution and concern into her name.

Her assistant's sigh came over the line. "I know, Georgia. *I know.*" She paused. "I just can't help myself. He makes me melt."

Unbidden, Georgia's gaze slid to Linc and her thoughts raced back to this morning, when he'd kissed her and *she'd* melted. Almost all over him, not to mention the parts of her that had more than melted, but simmered. Namely that secret place between her legs she'd desperately wanted to put closer to him.

She knew exactly what Karen was talking about because she was in lust with someone she shouldn't be lusting after, too. But sweet mercy, when that sinfully carnal mouth had touched hers, and the taste of him had exploded on her tongue…

Parts of Georgia had tingled she hadn't been aware even had nerve endings. Every single cell in her body had brightened significantly, as though they'd been hit with a power surge.

And they had, Georgia realized. They'd been hit with the voltage of Linc's megawatt sex appeal.

They'd been hit with *more*.

Unfortunately, rather than becoming accustomed to his touch and what it could do to her, Georgia seemed only to be getting worse. When he'd crouched down and looked at her tattoo this morning, she'd had to bite her bottom lip to keep from moaning aloud with pleasure. His fingers were warm and strong, and those mossy green eyes had darkened and dilated with heat when he'd looked up at her. He could have let her go, could have stopped doodling on her foot at any point after he'd realized it was a frog. But had he? No.

Though it could merely be insanity on her part, Georgia got the impression the same wild ignorant urge that currently had her under its thumb had knuckled Linc under, as well.

Georgia would like to chalk his interest up to her irresistibility, but figured a more likely reason lay in the fact that she didn't let him mow over her, and she wasn't constantly making gooey eyes at him. From what little time she'd spent in his company, she'd managed to peg what sort of woman he dated. She'd be beautiful, easily enamored and disposable. Georgia, who had no illusions about being beautiful, would admit to be a wee bit enamored, but would not allow herself to be disposable.

That was why she'd insisted on doing the fake dumping in their fake relationship. In the event that things got any more complicated between them— translate: she completely lost her mind and indulged in the *more* that had eluded her for her entire sexual life—then she'd be the one to call it quits, not him.

Though she'd like to think she could keep things purely casual between them, Georgia already knew better. There was that rush of sweet emotion that blanketed her heart every time he did something exasperating or boorish. It was the unexpected smile that tugged at her mouth when he said something politically incorrect. It was the way he had to touch everything to understand it.

That little character trait had been particularly evident this morning when they'd stopped by his loft. Georgia had remembered a lot in detail, but having the time to wander about while he changed and look at things, well…she'd been able to look deeper.

The studio, in particular, had been a treasure trove of discovery. Despite knocking her for being so organized, she'd noticed that Linc made sure to keep everything in its proper place, as well. The room had been neat and efficient, and the art…

There'd been something distinctly sensual about the pieces she'd seen. Smooth and rounded, heavy, but finely crafted. It had been all too easy to imagine him there at the wheel, shirtless, those strong hands molding and shaping, creating a work of art from a lump of clay.

From what she could tell he'd been experimenting with different finishes, as well. While most were cast in varying earth tones, there were also deep blues and aqua tones. She'd been especially drawn to a tall, curving vase in a compelling shade of green, eerily like his eyes.

Linc had caught her looking at it and had actually blushed. *Linc Stone—blush.* It boggled the mind. For someone to be so sure and certain about everything else, this little flash of vulnerability made him more…human somehow, for lack of a better term.

It was also much more dangerous.

He was more than just a badass bounty hunter,

more than just a gorgeous muscle-bound man with wonderful hands, a set of mouthwateringly large shoulders and six-pack abs. He was more than just a guitar-playing artist with a penchant for junk food and high-end electronics. He was more than a wicked smile and wicked sense of humor. He was more than just his father's son and Cade and Gracie's brother.

She watched him laugh at something Cade said and felt a small, sad smile slide cross her lips.

No, Linc Stone was a guy she could fall in love with—so much for *knowing* when she was in love, Georgia thought, more confused than ever—and somehow that was more terrifying than the possibility of never finding her mother's ring.

"SORRY WE'RE GETTING such a late start," Linc said, shooting a look at Georgia. She'd been strangely quiet since they'd gotten back on the road. "I didn't realize the photo shoot was going to take so long, otherwise I would have rescheduled."

"No problem," she assured him. "Taking care of that was important. Besides, it's not like we've been hot on his trail." She pulled a frown. "So far we haven't found the first clue."

Linc smiled at her. "You're not losing faith in me, are you?"

"Not in you, specifically," Georgia told him. "But

I'd be lying if I said I wasn't beginning to get a little discouraged."

"Georgia, we've only just started. This is the nature of the business. This is how it works. You watched Dog, didn't you?" he teased. Where had his determined, scrappy little fighter gone? Where was his stungun-toting wedding planner out for revenge? He hated that she was discouraged, hated that he couldn't magically fix things for her. It made him feel helpless and angry. "Did he find his guy the first place he looked?"

That brought her smile out of hiding. "No, but damned close. I think you'd have better luck if you grew your hair out into a mullet and wore reflective shades."

He glanced at her sexy curls. "I see you left yours down today."

"Well, I could hardly wear it in a ponytail after you told me I could hire out to haunt houses with it up," she said wryly.

"I didn't tell you that you could h-hire out to h-haunt houses," he said, chuckling under his breath. "I merely suggested that it looked better down."

A droll smile rolled across her lips and she feigned surprise. "Oh, really. 'It's ghastly' was only a 'suggestion'?"

"Hire out to haunt houses," Linc repeated, snorting. "You're a piece of work, you know that?"

"That's right," she said, nodding primly. "I'm a *master*piece."

Another unexpected laugh broke up in his throat and he reached over and slung an arm around her neck. "There we go," he said, dragging her closer to him. "My little smart-ass is back."

"Back to the name calling, are we, dickwad?"

Linc bit his tongue to keep from laughing again. "You have to stop calling me that."

"What?" she asked innocently. "You don't like it?"

"What's there to like about it?"

"Well, it's better than dickless, isn't it?"

"Georgia."

"Fine. I'll see if I can come up with something different."

"Excellent. Leave the word *dick* out of it, please."

She tsked under her breath. "Are you always so picky?"

He pulled into the Vacation Inn parking lot and turned to stare at her, purposely letting his gaze trail over her mouth long enough to make her lick her lips. "Believe it or not, Trouble, I am quite picky."

He had the pleasure of watching a nervous sigh slip from between those ripe lips. "There's nothing wrong with being particular, I suppose."

"Good. I'm glad we're on the same page." As though propelled by some hidden force, he leaned forward and brushed a whisper of a kiss across her lips. "Let's roll," he said. "And remember to—"

"Yeah, yeah, I know. Follow your lead."

"For the record, there's a different play for who's behind the counter. When a guy's behind the counter, you're going to be looking for Carter because you want to get laid."

From the corner of his eye, he watched Georgia's mouth drop open in outrage. "I— What?" She hurried to keep up with him.

Resisting the urge to smile, Linc peered through the plate glass door and saw a middle-aged blonde who looked like she'd seen her share of losers over the years. "You're in luck this time because it's a woman."

"How do I play it if it's a woman?" she asked suspiciously.

Linc grinned at her and reached for the door. "No worries. You're only pregnant."

Georgia stalled in the doorway and, mouth open once again, glared at him. "No, I'm not," she said through gritted teeth.

He nudged her forward. "Yes, you are. Now go ask if he's been here."

Mumbling something under her breath that sounded suspiciously like "dickhead," Georgia plastered a smile on her face and tentatively moved to the counter.

The clerk welcomed them with a pleasant, "Good afternoon," followed by the obligatory, "How can I help you?"

"Hi," Georgia replied nervously. "I was actually looking for someone and wondered if you'd seen him."

"Ma'am, our guest information is private," she said. "I'm sure you understand."

"I do, but if you could just take a look," Georgia said, using her most charming wedding-planner voice and sliding the photo across the counter. "I would really appreciate it. It's…important."

"Ma'am, I'm afraid that's against company policy. I wish I could help you, but I can't."

Time for him to interfere, Linc decided. He walked over and put his arm around Georgia, giving her a careful concerned squeeze. "It's all right, sis. We'll keep looking until we find him. And when we do, I'm going to *beat* enough child support out of him to last a lifetime." He glanced at the clerk, whose brow had furrowed, and nodded. "Thanks for your help, ma'am. Sorry we bothered you."

Georgia picked up the photo and, still nestled under his arm and playing the grieving-knocked-up-single-girl-in-search-of-the-lowlife-that-had-left-her, turned with him and started to walk away.

Three, two, one…

"Wait!"

They paused and turned around. "Yes?" Georgia asked hopefully.

The clerk sighed. "Let me take a look at that, would you?"

Georgia nodded and handed the picture over.

The woman studied the picture for a few seconds, then handed it back. "I've seen this guy before, but it's been a few days. He's not what you'd call a regular, but he's stayed here from time to time."

Linc pulled a card from his wallet and handed it to her. "Next time he comes in, we'd sure appreciate it if you gave us a call," he told her.

She nodded determinedly. "You can bet I will." She glanced at Georgia and a kind smile shaped her lips. "When are you due, sweetie?"

"August," Georgia said, smiling, though a shadow had moved across her eyes. "Thanks for your help."

Linc walked her back to the truck and opened the door for her. "Feel better?" he asked. "It's been a few days, but he's been here. It's the start we've been looking for."

"Do you think she'll really call when she realizes you're a bounty hunter?"

He frowned. "What do you mean?"

"Your card, genius," she said. "You gave her *your* card."

Linc chuckled. "Give me some credit, Trouble. I gave her *a* card, not *my* card. The one she's holding says I'm Lincoln Holbrook, general contractor."

Georgia smiled and inclined her head. "Forgive me for doubting you."

Linc nodded. "Damn straight." He closed her door, then joined her inside the truck.

"Lincoln Holbrook?" she asked. "Where'd that come from?"

"My birth certificate. I'm named after my grand-fathers." Intrigued, he slid her a glance. "What's your middle name?"

"Cecille. So what's next?"

Linc pulled into the all-night pancake house next to the hotel they'd just left and shifted into Park. Cecille, he thought, testing the name. It suited her. It was classy, like her.

"We start canvassing," he said. "Same plan, same story. He's been in the area. Now it's time to tighten the noose and run him to ground."

Her eyes twinkled and a slow smile tugged at her ripe lips. "You're in your element now, aren't you?"

Linc grinned and pulled a shrug. "Sweetheart, I'm *always* in my element. You just let a little doubt cloud your vision."

An exaggerated wrinkle developed between Georgia's brows. "How on earth do you carry it?"

"Carry what?"

"That enormous ego," she said. "It's got to weigh a ton."

Linc snorted. "Yeah, well, that streak of sarcasm you've got going on can't be easy to haul around, either."

"Sarcasm is light," she said.

"So is confidence." Linc studied her for a minute, ridiculously turned on as a result of this little verbal volley. "You know what I think?"

She blinked, feigning surprise. "You have thoughts? Seriously?"

"I think you argue with me because it makes you hot."

A startled chuckle broke up in her throat and she blushed adorably. "The weight of that ego has cracked your brain. I argue with you because it amuses me."

"Then why are your nipples hard?"

Georgia gasped and looked down at her chest. "My nipples aren't hard," she said, her voice oddly strangled.

"But you thought they were, or you wouldn't have looked." He gave her an up-nod and chewed the inside of his cheek. "Admit it. You want me."

She studied him for a moment, those smooth, dark eyes equally outraged and resigned. Though it had started out as a joke of sorts, Linc suddenly realized how important her answer was. Did he want her? More than his next breath. More than was prudent, particularly given the emotional tug to her he simply couldn't deny, not to mention his terrifying penchant for mentally dressing her in a damned wedding gown. But he couldn't seem to help himself, couldn't make himself not want her, and dammit, he wanted her to want him, as well. He wanted her to need him as much as he needed her. Which was ridiculous when he knew she was looking for a forever kind of thing, and he no longer knew what in the hell he was looking for.

He just knew he'd found her and, at the moment, that was all that mattered.

"I want lots of things, Linc," she finally said. "I want ice cream for breakfast and candy bars for lunch. I want to skip exercise class and play hooky from work. I want to stay up all night and sleep all day." She lifted a shoulder. "Like I said, I want a lot of things. But that doesn't make them good for me."

Unable to help himself, Linc felt a wicked chuckle bubble up his throat. He reached over and slipped the pad of his thumb over her distractingly sexy mouth. "Sweetheart, make no mistake, *I* would be good for you."

But he grimly suspected she'd ultimately be the death of him.

10

MAKE NO MISTAKE. I'd *be good for you.*

Despite the fact they'd spent all day and a good portion of the evening hitting all of the hotels, restaurants and coffee shops in the airport area looking for Carter—or any sign of Carter—and despite the fact that she'd rehearsed the whole poor-pregnant-me spiel until she almost believed it herself, those words from Linc had haunted her all damned day.

Because she knew they were true.

In the sexual sense, anyway, which was exactly how he meant it, the sneaky bastard.

Now, here they were, at the end of another day and rather than looking forward to her bath and bed, she was loath to see him go.

Why? Georgia asked herself. Because clearly she was an ignorant glutton for punishment who couldn't control her basic instincts. Furthermore, as ridiculous as it sounded, if Linc was right and Carter was just out of grasp, then though she'd hopefully have her mother's ring back…her time with Linc would be up. Just a few days ago that would have suited her perfectly, but now… Now, as goofy and improbable as it sounded, she'd miss him.

"Does your brother often stand at his door and watch for you to come home?" Linc asked as they drove past Jack's house.

Georgia chuckled tiredly. "Er…no. He's got Karen spying on me. I told her to call him and let him know that I'd be coming home soon."

He shook his head and his gaze tangled with hers. The dashlights illuminated that beautiful masculine profile. He had the most amazing bone structure, Georgia thought. As finely crafted as those pieces of pottery he molded. "So the whole guardian thing is for my benefit then?"

She smiled. "He perceives you as a threat. I wonder what ever would have given him that idea," she mused dramatically. Her eyes rounded. "Oh, wait. You told him you were my *boyfriend.*"

Linc hummed under his breath and pulled his SUV up behind her car. "I wonder what he's going to say then when I spend the night."

Georgia's mouth parched. She knew it was inevitable. Knew she wanted him to stay. That this was going to happen. "S-spend the night?"

"It's late. I'm tired." A slow smile tugged at the

corner of his mouth. "I was hoping for a little southern hospitality."

They both knew he was hoping for more than that, but rather than point it out, Georgia decided she should battle the almost irresistible urge to squirm in her seat. He was giving her an out, she knew. Letting her know that if she didn't want this to happen she could simply refuse and life as they knew it would continue to exist. He could have kissed her and she would have forgotten to protest. He could have taken advantage of her own desire, but instead he'd put the ball firmly in her court.

Because, at the end of the day, her badass bounty hunter was a gentleman.

And that, Georgia decided, combined with the *more* she so desperately wanted, was a gesture that she couldn't and didn't want to refuse. A wicked thrill of anticipation moved through her.

"Do you have clothes?"

He smiled, the grin packing enough heat to raise the temperature in the cab a good ten degrees. "I'm a bounty hunter, Trouble. I'm always prepared."

Her belly fluttered. "I thought that was the Boy Scouts."

He grunted and reached for a bag in the back. "Boy Scouts are pansies."

Another politically incorrect, boorish thing to say

and yet she found it thrillingly adorable. God help her, she was losing her mind…and possibly another significant organ if she wasn't careful.

"Come on," he said. "You can show me to my room."

Her stomach a ball of nerves, palms tingling, Georgia unlocked her back door and set her purse upon the counter. Stitch, Bogey and Bacall came running to inspect who'd arrived, but quickly lost interest when Georgia didn't immediately move to feed them.

She shot Linc a pointed look and quirked a brow. "You mean you weren't planning on staying in mine?"

Evidently caught, he merely grinned. "Only if I was invited." He sidled closer and nuzzled the side of her neck, setting off a flash fire of goose bumps. "Am I invited, Trouble?" he asked roughly, his voice a decadent masculine purr.

Funny that she could smile knowing she was damned, Georgia thought, but what the hell? In answer, she slipped her hands beneath his sweater and uttered a little gasp of pleasure when her fingers found warm, supple skin.

Smiling, Linc found her mouth, sucked at her bottom lip. "I'll take that as a yes."

"Meet me upstairs in five minutes," Georgia told him. "My bedroom is the first door on the right." Though it felt like she'd been waiting a lifetime for this moment, Georgia refused to let herself get so caught up—which was damned difficult when she could have been eternally happy for him to take her right here on the kitchen floor—that she didn't make the most of it.

The most of *more.*

If she and Linc were going to do this—and *thrillingly* they were—then she wanted to do it right. She wanted to savor every moment. She wanted to seduce and be seduced. The blood hammering in her veins screamed *now!now!now!* but she wanted more than just an orgasm, Georgia thought.

She wanted him.

Hot and naked and needy, in her bed, desperate for her. She wanted those big strong hands sliding over her body, kneading and warm, massaging her breasts and slipping between her thighs.

She reluctantly withdrew from his embrace and hurried upstairs. She lit a candle, freshened up, then changed into a sheer robe that barely brushed the tops of her thighs. She considered a thong, but remembering Linc's comment this morning about naked being best, she abstained. The robe, she decided, he'd simply have to deal with. She was relatively confident in her sexual ability, but those body issues wouldn't go away quite so easily.

She stood in the middle of the room, waiting for

him when he finally sauntered in. He'd removed his shirt and shoes, but had left his jeans on, the waist unsnapped.

Her mouth parched.

Linc's hot gaze slid over the sheer robe, lingering over her nipples, sliding down her belly, the heart of her sex, then his gaze bumped back up to hers. "You're beautiful," he murmured thickly, unwittingly bringing a blush of pleasure to her face.

"I know I'm not beautiful, but if I pass muster then that's good enough for me."

He stared at her, that dark green gaze sharpening perceptively. "Don't argue with me," he told her, sidling forward. He slipped his finger into the sash and pulled, revealing her naked body to his hungry gaze. "When I say you're beautiful, then I mean you're beautiful."

He did mean it, Georgia realized, her racing heart skipping a beat of pleasure. "You're not half-bad yourself."

A wicked smile hovered on his lips, he bent and pressed a kiss to her jaw, slid his hands over her sides—hot, sure and seductive—then reached around, molding his hands to her rump, and squeezed. "I know," he said.

Leaning toward him, Georgia chuckled. "You're so full of—"

Linc kissed her before she could finish the insult. His tongue darted in and out of her mouth, slowly, druggingly, his lips sliding over hers, creating a delicious friction between their joined mouths. Her bare nipples tingled and budded against his chest and a rush of warmth coated her aching folds as he pulled her even closer to him. The robe sagged open, revealing her naked body and his jeans abraded her bare skin, making her mewl with pleasure.

She slid her hands over his chest, thumbed his male nipples, then tested the bulk of his shoulders beneath her palms. God, he felt good. Warm skin, supple muscle, sleek and perfectly formed, as though just for her pleasure.

The mere idea made her breath leak out of her lungs in a shuddering exhale of anticipation. She smoothed her hands over his rib cage, memorizing every bump and ridge, then finally his over his taut belly.

Unable to stand the fact that she was basically naked and he still relatively dressed, she found the zipper and sucked his tongue into her mouth as she dragged it down. Linc groaned as she slipped her hands beneath the waistband of his briefs and pushed them down over his hips. He kicked them off from around his feet and she felt the part of him she'd been craving nudge impatiently against her belly.

She wrapped her hand around him, felt him jerk against her palm.

"Trouble," he growled.

"Shh," she said, working the hot, slippery skin against her hand. He was huge, Georgia thought, almost drunk and giddy with need. Just like the rest of him. She'd known, of course. Logic had told her to expect this part of him to be of a proportionate size, but knowing it and feeling it were two completely different things.

And tasting it, she knew, would be another altogether. She dropped to her knees, looked up at Linc, then swirled her tongue over the head of his engorged penis.

His eyes darkened and she thought she heard his teeth crack.

She sucked him into her mouth, dragged the whole of him in. He felt wonderful against her tongue, hot and soft, alive and ready.

Linc swore through gritted teeth and pushed his hands into her hair, seemingly holding her in place, afraid that she'd stop.

She made another deep pull and sucked hard to let him know he needn't have worried. She felt his thighs tense and played with his balls, worked the slippery skin with her hand all the while sucking him, eating him, savoring every inch of him in her mouth.

A steady throb built between her legs, her nipples tingled and she felt her sex ripen, readying for him.

"Enough," Linc finally told her, dragging her to her feet and propelling her toward the bed. "It's my turn to taste you." That hungry gaze slid over her, leaving a scorching path in its wake as he landed on the mattress alongside of her.

"Fine," she said. "Eat me."

His eyes widened and a wicked chuckle eddied up his throat. He slid his finger under and over the curve of both breasts, tracing her before cupping her fully in hand and thumbing her aching nipple. She winced with pleasure, then moaned as his hot mouth latched upon her peak. He nibbled and sucked, laved and lingered, tasting and testing every part of her. His hands were all over her, learning every curve, every indentation, every inch of skin. It was as though she were a piece of clay, him the potter, feeling and memorizing, testing and shaping, and she got the vague idea of what it felt like to literally be putty in his hands.

Linc kissed his way down her belly making little masculine purrs of pleasure, stopping to linger around her navel as his fingers suddenly slid over the top of her thigh, then inside to part her curls.

The first brush of his fingers against her made her back arch off the sheet. Georgia gasped as sensation bolted through her. It was as though every hot spot in her body had been hit with a surge. Her nipples tightened even more, and her feminine muscles clenched, a silent plea for more.

"So wet," he murmured thickly. "God, I bet you taste good," he said, then looked up and smiled at her. "And you told me to eat you, so…" He was suddenly there, feasting between her legs. He slipped his tongue over her hot, weeping folds.

Unexpected pleasure bolted through her and she cried out, shocked and boneless and miserably aware of how much she'd been missing her entire life. Linc pushed a finger deep inside of her and hooked it around, hitting upon a hidden spot that made her vision blacken around the edges. He laved her clit and pressed his thumb against the tightened rosebud of her bottom, causing a firework of sensation to detonate in her loins.

She thrashed beneath him. "Linc, I—"

He licked harder, forming a vee with his tongue that did the most amazing things to her. She could feel herself hovering on the brink of orgasm; knew it was coming.

Evidently Linc did, too. He slowed, having primed her enough, she supposed, and retrieved a condom from his pants.

"You were prepared," Georgia said as he tore the package open with his teeth.

"Hopeful," Linc corrected. "I was hopeful."

For whatever reason, the comment warmed her heart and made her chest ache with an unnamed joy that had no business being there. Especially now. Georgia knew the second she allowed Linc into her body she would become just like those other girls he'd dated—disposable—and while her heart pricked with disappointment...she just couldn't help herself. She wanted this.

She wanted *him*.

He swiftly rolled the protection into place, then positioned himself at her center. He nudged, begging admittance as his heavy-lidded gaze tangled with hers. Even now, he would stop, she realized. Even now, as they hovered on the precipice of an irrevocable change, he would still give her the choice.

She bent forward and licked his nipple, then arched her hips up beneath his, forcing him inside of her. Her breath left her in a long whoosh and she tensed around him, holding him inside as he filled her up.

"Are you going to follow my lead or not?" Georgia asked him, throwing his line right back at him.

Linc chuckled. He deliberately withdrew, making her wince and reach for him, then pushed back inside of her, filling her up once more.

He bent and pulled a tingling peak deep into his

mouth. She felt that tug all the way down to her womb, and a smothered, keening cry tore from her throat.

"Sweet heaven," Georgia muttered, her belly deflating, her neck arching away from the bed. She was rigid and boneless, mindless and euphoric.

"You smell good," Linc told her, laving her nipple. "Like strawberries." He made a masculine purr of pleasure, then licked a path to her other breast and sampled it, as well, all the while pushing in and out of her, slow, steady thrusts that were gradually stoking a fire that was already burning out of control.

Unable to help herself, Georgia upped the tempo between them. She drew her legs back and anchored them around his hips, then pushed up, gratified when she felt his balls slap at her aching flesh.

"Mercy," she growled through gritted teeth.

Evidently the bold move snapped the fine line of Linc's control and he lashed an arm around her waist, dragged her up even farther against him and pounded into her. Gone was the gentle lover, and in his place was a man who'd lost it.

With her.

For her.

Georgia felt a wild laugh bubble up her throat as joy and pleasure ripped through her. He pumped harder, faster, then faster still, pushing her farther

and farther toward the brass ring of release. It was
hovering just out of reach, just beyond the next wonderful, mind-bending, back-clawing thrust of him
deep inside of her. She loved the delicious draw and
drag between their bodies. He was so big, so splen-
didly proportioned and something about having this
man at her fingertips caused her heart to threaten to
beat right out of her chest.

"Linc, I need— I want—"

Her breath came in little short gasps ripped from
her burning lungs and her thighs tensed as she finally
reached the end of the world—not to mention the
mattress, Georgia thought dimly.

He reached down between their joined bodies and
massaged her clit, sending her abruptly over the edge
of reason and right into the waiting arms of the most
amazing release.

The orgasm swept her under, then lifted her up.
It circled in on itself, tightening and tightening until
a single bright light burst behind her eyelids, momentarily blinding her. A buzzing noise rang in her
ears and every nerve ending celebrated in pure,
unadulterated joy.

That was it, Georgia thought, a giddy chuckle
breaking up in her throat as he continued to milk the
orgasm through every lingering contraction.

She'd just experienced the *more*...and didn't

know how she'd ever be able to settle for less now that she'd had it.

Follow his lead, indeed, she thought. Right now she'd follow him to the ends of the earth.

DARK CURLY HAIR fanned out around her head, melting chocolate eyes, lush, ripe mouth open in a soundless scream of pleasure, rosy nipples absorbing the force of his thrusts, her welcoming body clinging to his…

If he'd ever seen anything more beautiful, more amazing, sexier in his entire life, Linc Stone couldn't recall it.

Georgia Hart, in the throes of a back-bending, ass-clawing, soundless screaming orgasm, was hands-down the most gorgeous woman he'd ever seen in his life, and if he lived to be a thousand, that would never change. The picture she made right now would be permanently etched on his memory.

Initially Linc had intended to take things slow, but feeling her legs tighten around him, her greedy body sucking him in and contracting around him…Linc had simply lost control. Odd, when that had never happened before, but Georgia Hart had a way of pushing buttons he didn't know existed. It had been foolish to think that it wouldn't happen here, as well, and he knew that mining that little nugget of truth would result in some unhappy realizations he'd just as soon not deal with at the moment.

So he wouldn't.

Instead, he would savor every inch of her, fill her up, then empty her out again, because he simply couldn't help himself. She was the light to his dark, the yin to his yang, the answer and the prayer.

She was it, a little heeded voice whispered, one he chose to ignore.

Linc winced as she tightened around him again and again, the force of her release coming dangerously close to triggering his own. Feeling his body prime for orgasm, he pumped harder and faster, harder and faster, then faster still. Her rosy nipples beckoned and he bent down and pulled one puckered bud into his mouth, the taste of her melting over his tongue. He growled low in his throat.

So sweet, he thought. So unbearably sweet…

He pounded into her greedy body, pushed and pushed until he was certain that he was going to take her right off the bed. They'd certainly gotten too damned close to the edge, that was for sure.

"Linc, I— It's happening again," she said brokenly. She winced from the pleasure and pain of it. Made feminine mewling sounds that made his chest ache they were so damned welcome. "I don't know if I can take—"

He chuckled knowingly and angled deeper. "Oh, trust me. You can."

She whimpered, and clung to him, muttering strings of broken, nonsensical madness brought on by sheer pleasure. Pleasure that he was giving her.

Just him.

The mere idea made him want to pound his chest and roar. There was something so important—so right on an elemental level with that thought that Linc felt a strange kind of peace wash over him, followed by a irrational dart of unknown panic he knew better than to explore.

Thankfully, he didn't have to because she was hot and womanly and for the moment, his, and he wanted nothing more than to lose himself completely inside of her, to forget that she was mouthy and opinionated and believed in happily-ever-after. To forget that there was a faceless groom out there just waiting to take her from him. Bastard, Linc thought. He couldn't have her. He wouldn't let him.

Because he wanted her.

Georgia pumped and flexed harder against him, her breathing becoming increasingly ragged once more. "You'd better— I need— *Oh, dammit!*"

Another scream tore from her throat and she arched violently against him, thrusting those beautiful breasts up, that sweet belly quivering. Her thighs quaked and her breath came in jagged little gasps as she clamped around him again and again.

Without warning, he came hard.

Another first, Linc thought dimly. The orgasm blasted from his loins with enough force to blow the end out of the condom, but at the moment he didn't give a damn.

He couldn't. Cognitive thought escaped him.

Georgia was all dewy and melting beneath him, her eyes dark and sated, her lips plump and wet. He locked his knees and nudged deep, digging his toes firmly into the mattress to keep himself as deep inside of her as possible.

Given the choice, he believed he'd just stay right here forever, locked inside her, savoring her goodness.

Breathing hard, he kissed her cheek and settled his forehead against hers. "God, woman, you're going to be the death of me."

She chuckled, flexed around him once more. "You say that as if it were a bad thing."

Linc carefully withdrew, snagged a tissue from the box next to the bed and disposed of the condom. He rolled back onto his side and tugged her with him. The scent of strawberries, lemon furniture polish and sex perfumed the air, bringing a smile to his lips.

"I'm not ready to die yet." He traced a figure-eight on her upper arm. "Even though it would be one helluva way to go."

She let go a dramatic sigh and wiggled closer to him, snuggling tight. She was a perfect fit, Linc realized, curiously warmed by the thought. Her head just fit between his shoulder and chin. Ordinarily he didn't like to linger in bed, but with Georgia it seemed like the natural segue.

"I sure am glad you invited yourself over to spend the night."

He felt a tired smile roll over his lips. "I sure am glad that you let me." He gave her a squeeze. "This is nice."

She leaned up on her elbow and an idea twinkled in her sweet gaze. "You know what would be even nicer?"

He quirked a brow. "Having sex again?"

"That, too…but I was thinking about something else."

"Oh, really?"

"Really." She pressed a kiss against his jaw, inadvertently initiating his launch sequence once more. "How does a bath sound to you?"

An image of the two of them sinking into that claw-foot tub outside materialized all too readily in Linc's mind. Wet rump, wet breasts and pouting nipples. Steam rising off the water. Curls and soft mewling sighs.

He wrapped a strand of her hair around his finger and tugged her close for a kiss. "I like that idea."

"Good," she said, smiling, her lids at half-mast. "Cause you're going to follow my lead this time."

11

"ARE YOU CERTAIN your brother isn't going to mind if I ride one of his horses?"

Georgia finished tightening the saddle on Jeremiah and felt a droll smile roll around her lips. "If he didn't sneak over this morning and shoot you for riding his sister last night, then I'm guessing you should be all right."

A shocked chuckle rumbled up Linc's throat. "You're wicked, you know that?"

She climbed up onto Mags's back and grinned at him, entirely too pleased and sated this morning, but unable to resist the temptation of being happy. "You might have mentioned it once or twice. Or twenty." She gestured to his horse. "Are you going to stare at him or ride him?"

"It's been a while since I've ridden," he admitted. "But fine. Game on, then." As though he'd been reared in the saddle, Linc smoothly landed on Jeremiah's back and settled his other foot unerringly into the stirrup. He held the reins with a natural ease in one hand and leaned forward and stroked the horse's neck with the other. Jeremiah whinnied with horsey pleasure.

See? Georgia thought, shaking her head. Even the damned horse wasn't immune to his touch.

Linc caught her staring and smiled, the easy grin making her stomach flutter with warmth and some foolhardy emotion which had no place in this disposable arrangement they currently found themselves in. "What?" he asked.

"Nothing. Come on," she said. "We're burning daylight."

"We're not burning much of it," Linc told her. "The sun isn't even completely up yet."

Georgia nudged Mags into a canter. "That's the best time to ride."

And it was. There was nothing quite like watching the birth of a new day, the sun's first rays kissing the creek that ran along the back of their property. Between the warm fall colors and the bright orange promise of a magnificent dawn, there was something almost spiritual about the experience, particularly when viewed from horseback.

Linc fell in behind her, thankfully letting her take the lead this morning. Not that he hadn't last night, as well, she thought, remembering their extended bath.

Sweet mercy.

She'd only *thought* she'd been satisfied.

Linc had built a fire while she ran their bath and they'd settled into the hot bubbly water and enjoyed a nice long soak, followed by even better nice long sex. After the initial edge had been taken off, she'd found that she wasn't as impatient as she'd been up in the bedroom. After the bath, she'd had time to explore.

For instance, she'd discovered she loved the hollow indentation of his spine, that vulnerable area where neck met shoulder, the sleek line of his back illuminated in the firelight.

She'd discovered that his hair had golden streaks in it when the light struck it just right, and that his eyes were speckled with golden flecks when he was turned on.

What she hadn't learned—and what she intended to find out—was why he was so opposed to falling in love. It wasn't so much marriage that he didn't care for, Georgia had realized, so much as it was the idea of giving his heart to another person.

That had become glaringly evident yesterday when he'd made the fools-fall-in-love-only-complete-idiots-get married comment. Marriage was merely guilty by association. Love, for whatever reason—probably some crack-brained male thing— was the culprit.

Intuition told her that he expected her to pry because they had been intimate, so she knew better than to take that tack. At some point she hoped he would provide another unwitting insight. If he didn't, then naturally she would figure out a way to broach the subject because she was a woman who believed in love and wanted to help him revise his opinion.

In the meantime, she just wanted to enjoy being with him. Time was limited, after all, of that she was certain, and if she allowed herself to dwell on it she'd become morose and miserable, which was out of the question.

Used to the route, Mags naturally came to a stop as they crested the small hill. The creek and valley below lay out before them, the first fingers of dawn inching over the horizon. From beside her, Linc whistled low.

"Wow," he breathed quietly.

Georgia merely nodded. "This is why I'm relaxed in the mornings," she said. "I can come out here, me and Mags, and can see just where I fit in the grand scheme of things. I'm just a little speck in this big old world, Linc. But I like to think it's a significant speck. I know that I'm not finding a cure for cancer or pioneering space technology, but I believe that I make a difference in people's lives, and ultimately, in the world."

"Well, of course you do," he told her. "We all make a difference in one form or another."

She shot him a wry smile. "Even those of us who help those fools who fell in love become idiots who marry?"

Linc swore and looked away. "Sorry about that," he said sheepishly. He grimaced. "It was a shitty thing to say."

"Yeah, but at least you're honest. You wouldn't have said it if you didn't believe it." She chuckled softly. "You're funny that way. It's refreshing."

A bark of dry laughter erupted from his throat. "Only you would think that. Everyone else thinks I'm an opinionated, tactless ass."

She nodded. "Well you're that, too, but one doesn't negate the other."

He smiled at her, those mossy green eyes golden in the sunlight. "Thanks. I think." He paused. "You know what I like about you, Georgia?"

"You mean aside from my ass?" she teased. That had been particularly gratifying. She'd always worried over the size of her rear end, but Linc had seemed especially taken with it.

His eyes darkened. "Yes, aside from your ass, though it is damned wonderful," he added. His gaze searched hers. "I like that you're genuine. What you see is what you get with you, isn't it?"

"For the most part," she admitted, pleased. "I have to walk a fine line when I'm working." She rolled her eyes. "Compromise is a big part of what I do. But if I feel strongly about something, I'll fight for it." Mags shifted beneath her and she smiled. "Besides, being genuine is a lot more efficient than putting the effort into being someone you're not, right?"

Linc chuckled. "And there's always that." He paused and those green eyes lit with some unreadable emotion. "My mom would have liked you," he said.

Another blanket of warmth settled over her heart and she stilled, sensing that he was about to share something significant with her. "Yeah?"

"Yeah. She appreciated directness, too." He laughed and his gaze turned inward. "And she was efficient. It's funny the things you remember, you know? When I was little, I loved helping her hang out the clothes. She'd always pin things together, all the way down the line. Every day was an adventure. We'd take picnics and go to the creek, we'd play in the rain." He chuckled. "She never missed an opportunity to make a day special."

"She sounds like an amazing woman. I wish I could have met her."

"She *was* an amazing woman, and I only appre-

ciate that more the older I get. My dad..." He shook
his head. "My dad just about lost his mind when she
died."

"What happened?"

"Car wreck," Linc told her, his lips twisted with
bitter humor. "Sixteen-year-old kid with a shiny new
license, a shiny new car and virtually no experience.
My dad lost his wife, we lost our mother, and those
parents lost their child."

Her heart aching, she winced. "Oh, Linc," she
breathed. "That's terrible."

Linc idly toyed with the reins. "What was terrible
was watching my dad go from a larger-than-life in-
domitable man to a broken-hearted empty shell of a
human being in the blink of an eye. If it hadn't been
for Cade, we would have ended up in foster care. He
took care of us while my Dad struggled to pull
himself together."

That, clearly, was the glossed-over version, Georgia thought, her heart aching for the boy he'd been.
"How old were you?"

"Twelve."

So he was old enough to know what was going on,
but not old enough to try and help, to do anything
about it. He would have been angry and heartbroken,
Georgia thought. Angry, heartbroken and impres-
sionable.

"I'm sorry, Linc," Georgia said, compelled to offer her sympathies.

"My dad worshipped the ground she walked on," he said. "You know what I remember most about them?"

"What?"

"They loved to dance," he said, smiling softly. "No matter what happened, at the end of the day, after supper, Dad would turn on Otis Redding— *always Otis*—and they'd slow dance in the living room." He chuckled. "Naturally Cade and I thought it was gross, but Gracie always got a moony smile on her face."

"Moony smile?" Georgia parroted, feigning outrage.

He rolled his eyes. "Girls. Always looking at things through your romance-colored glasses."

Georgia hesitated. "You know she's really going to miss her mother when we start planning her wedding, right?"

Linc nodded. "I know. She's gotten pretty close to our secretary, so I imagine she'll sort of step in and do some of those motherly things."

Georgia smiled. "You mean Marlene?"

He shot her a look and his eyes widened perceptibly. "That's right. I'd forgotten that you'd met her."

"She's a sweet woman."

Linc inclined his head. "She is sweet, but don't let her fool you. She can be tough when she needs to be."

Georgia snorted. "Any woman would have to have nerves of steel to work with all of you."

"Hey," Linc said, shooting her a scolding look. "Are you saying that you haven't found me a pleasure to work with?"

She poked her tongue in her cheek and resisted the urge to smile. "When you're not throwing Danishes out the car window, insinuating that I am a horny whore looking for my sugar daddy or I'm a knocked-up unwed mother, then yes, other than those times, you are a sheer joy."

"I sure didn't hear any complaints last night," Linc said smugly, displaying that beastly male arrogance that was at once annoying and thrilling. The man had testosterone in spades, Georgia decided. And only she would find that absolutely thrilling.

"If we hurry up, you won't hear any complaints again this morning," she told him.

Linc's gaze sharpened and a wicked chuckle bubbled up his throat. "Are you saying you're a sure thing, Trouble?"

Georgia let her gaze drift slowly over him and felt an arrow of heat land in her increasingly muddled womb. The man simply didn't have any idea how potent he was, which was intoxicating in and of itself. Long denim-encased legs, impossibly wide shoulders, those wonderful magical hands that had brought her so much pleasure last night, the achingly familiar line of his jaw and those unwittingly expressive mossy green eyes.

God, he was beautiful.

And she wasn't going to say a word, sure thing or otherwise, because she grimly suspected she'd share something stupid.

Like the fact that she'd quite possibly—at some point or another over the past few days, maybe even last night or right now at this very moment—fallen head over heels in love with him.

She'd been wrong. It hadn't been love at first sight, it hadn't hit her like a tidal wave the way she'd expected it. Instead, it had simply snuck up on her and happened when she wasn't looking.

No wonder they said love was blind.

"I THOUGHT YOU SAID we were tightening the noose," Georgia said, hours later as they pulled out of the final hotel parking lot.

He slid her a sidelong glance. "Patience isn't one of your virtues is it?"

"You know the answer to that already. Karen told you how I feel about 'downtime.'"

Linc chuckled. "This isn't downtime. This is just

part of the hurry-up-and-wait process. We've gone everywhere we know to go, right?"

"I suppose."

"We've checked off every item on your list and mine. We know he's been at the Vacation Inn, the Sleep Tight Travel Lodge and that he stiffed a meal at the Pancake Emporium, so he's still in town. We've given out cards, we've watched those places and the surrounding area that we know he's been. Now, we have to wait. It's how the game is played."

Georgia released a pent-up sigh. "I know that. And I know that you know what you're doing, so don't take my neuroses as failure on your part."

He grinned at her. "Don't worry. I'm not."

Frankly, aside from playing the guitar, throwing a cool pot and making a woman come, Linc didn't claim expertise on anything, but he knew he was damned good at his job. Georgia knew it, too, but her obsessive desire to make the most of every minute wasn't conducive to the bail bond business.

"So now what?" she asked.

"Ordinarily I would work on another case, but I was thinking we'd do something fun instead."

She blinked at him, clearly startled. "Fun?"

Though he knew he shouldn't, he laughed at her. "Yes, Trouble. *Fun.* You know, enjoy ourselves." Naturally that would involve him having sex with her at some point today—because he wouldn't be able to keep his hands off of her, of course—but he just wanted to be with her. To do something special for her. Why? He wouldn't answer that, though he knew it was important.

"I know what it means, I'm just not so sure we should be doing it."

"Why not?"

"Because we should be working."

A thought struck and he stared at her. "When was the last time you took a vacation?"

She flushed and twisted in her seat. "I don't know. It's been a while."

"How long a while?"

She frowned and looked away. "A good while."

"Georgia."

"I went to the beach when I graduated from college," she admitted finally.

Linc did a double take. "When you graduated from— How long ago was that? Five, six years?"

"Seven," she said. "I skipped a couple of grades in school."

Astounded, Linc couldn't let it go. "You haven't taken a vacation in seven years?"

"I believe we've covered that."

"Why the hell not?"

"My line of work never really experiences lull," she said. "I've always got something going on."

"My work doesn't experience a lull, either, but I still take a vacation every year."

"I suppose it's good for some people."

"Vacations are good for everybody, Trouble, not just 'some people.'" He cast her another glance and gave his head a little shake. "That settles it. We're having fun today. Think of it as a mini-vacation."

She winced regrettably. "You know, as wonderful as that sounds—"

He could tell she thought it was the opposite of wonderful.

"—if we aren't going to be looking for Carter, I should really log in some time at the store."

"No."

Her eyes widened. "No? What do you mean no?"

"No means no. It's not difficult. Karen is there. I'm sure you've blocked off this week to take care of this Carter issue and you're too damned efficient not to have taken care of everything that was going to need your attention until then."

"But I—

"You set your own trap, sweetheart," he said, tsking as though it were a shame when it really wasn't. "If you were a screwup like the rest of us, you'd have a leg to stand on. As it is, you don't." He reached over, threaded his fingers through hers and squeezed. Heat circled his heart and landed in his groin. "Now get ready to have some fun."

Seemingly resigned, Georgia's hand relaxed in his and a wry smile tugged the corner of her mouth. "I don't suppose I have a choice."

"No, you don't."

"So where are we going to have this mysterious fun?" she asked ominously.

"Well, first I thought we'd stop by a local crack house, then we'd—

"Crack house?"

He chuckled. "I'm kidding. Don't worry," he said, shooting her a smile. "We're going to stay right here in Memphis. Our fair city has a lot to offer and for some reason I get the impression that you've missed a lot of its attractions." He smiled when she didn't argue, silently affirming his fears.

Seven years since she'd had a vacation, Linc thought again. How was it that she could spend so much time making sure that everyone else found their joy but didn't seem as interested in finding her own? Honestly, the woman took driven to a whole new level. But then, just looking at the level of success she'd achieved at such a relatively young age explained that. She'd obviously been working her ass off.

Linc wheeled his SUV into a parking lot, found a spot near the gate and shifted into Park. Georgia peered through the windshield and a slow smile slid across her lips, infecting her whole face. Something in his chest shifted and tightened, momentarily making it difficult for him to breathe. He'd made the right choice in bringing her here, Linc thought, secretly pleased. Given her love of animals, it only seemed fitting. Hell, only Georgia Hart would have an incontinent, diaper-wearing, one-eyed dog.

"First stop on our Tour de Fun," Linc said, "the zoo."

And if he was lucky, they'd get to demonstrate some of their own animalistic tendencies.

12

"I CAN'T BELIEVE YOU are a hometown girl and have never been to Graceland, eaten a fried peanut butter and banana sandwich or ridden The Ducks. And don't even get me started on not giving Beale Street a try. It's the blues capital of the world, and you've never even heard of W.C. Handy." He shook his head as though it were a crying shame.

"I can't believe you keep saying you can't believe it," Georgia told him, smiling. "I've seen enough Elvis documentaries to know what Graceland is all about, though I do appreciate you taking me." She poked her tongue in her cheek. "Seeing the infamous Jungle Room in person was quite a treat."

He'd also walked up behind her while they'd been standing by the Jungle Room and told her in no uncertain terms what he'd like to do to her in there. Or anywhere, for that matter, which had sent a wicked thrill whipping through her.

Much like the one she was experiencing now,

Georgia thought, remembering the wonderful things Linc had done to her body last night.

And she wanted them again and again.

"As for the fried peanut butter and banana sandwich, I had no idea I was missing out on something so fabulous." She nodded succinctly. "I stand corrected."

"Beale Street?"

She paused consideringly, sorting through her impressions. "The guy doing the gymnastics in the middle of the street was quite cool." They'd wandered in and out of the shops, looking at everything from tacky sunglasses to old albums. Musicians were on every corner, cranking out their soulful sounds. Linc, she knew, was right in his element and several of the street players knew him. At one point he'd even been asked to step in while another player went to the bathroom. Watching those wonderful fingers competently stroking those strings, pulling the notes out of the guitar, his longish espresso curls falling across his cheek as the music moved out of him... Georgia released a shuddering breath.

That had been damned sexy.

She knew what those fingers felt like, how well they stroked, and the notes of sensual melody he'd pulled from her just this morning.

"The zoo?" Linc asked, interrupting her X-rated musings.

Georgia's heart blushed with pleasure. "I *loved* the zoo." It had been years and years since she'd been. In fact, if she wasn't mistaken the last time she'd been to the zoo had been with her Girl Scout troop in sixth grade. Maybe it had been seventh.

At any rate, she and Linc had strolled from one exhibit to the next, hand in hand, and had even gotten to take a little behind-the-scenes tour to see how much care and attention went into preparing the animals' food. It had been quite interesting, to say the least.

Her favorite thing, of course, had been the giant pandas. They were big and beautiful with their masked faces and sad eyes. Interestingly, there were only four pairs of giant pandas currently in the U.S.—less than a thousand in the world—and seeing one had been a unique opportunity she was glad she'd gotten the chance to have. Her gaze slid to Linc, she sighed softly, and her heart melted all over again.

Thanks to him.

She knew he'd been appalled by the fact that she hadn't taken a vacation, but frankly, Georgia had just always preferred to work. Though she enjoyed her own company for the most part, a vacation had always felt like a couples' thing and since she'd never really been part of a couple, she'd just put it off.

If she'd learned anything today—aside from the fact that she adored Linc Stone—she'd learned that she needed to change her thinking. Yes, going on a vacation with him would be a lot more fun, but whether she went as part of a couple or alone, she needed to make the time to do more things for herself. Soaking in her tub and taking a morning ride with Mags wasn't enough.

Furthermore, Linc had been right. Karen was fully capable of helping out more—craved more—but Georgia had always been such a micromanager she'd never given Karen the responsibility she was clearly ready for.

That would change.

She'd had *fun* today. To think that she'd been so reluctant to do this and yet, she'd truly enjoyed herself.

She squeezed Linc's hand and rested her head upon his shoulder as the Duck they were riding in made its way back to town. Another interesting experience, Georgia thought. The Ducks were amphibious vehicles that were originally built and used in World War Two. The Ducks of Memphis took a historical tour through the town by Sun Records, Saint Jude's Children's Research Center, the Pyramid and much more, then splashed into the backwaters of the Mississippi into the Wolf River Harbor.

They'd also found out the people who ran the

company were instrumental in helping the with the search and rescue of Hurricane Katrina victims. Just another tidbit that she'd learned during her Tour de Fun with Linc.

The tour guide finished his spiel and people began filing off the bus. Linc tossed a few bills into the tip bucket, then carefully helped her down. She landed against his front and had to resist the urge to go up on her tiptoe and kiss him. He was big and warm and smelled like fresh air, sexy man and patchouli.

His heavy-lidded gaze tangled with hers. "Where to now, Trouble?" he asked, that deep baritone moving through her much as the music had left his fingers.

Heat broadsided her, her belly went all hot and muddled and she felt her breasts pucker beneath the flimsy fabric of her bra.

She'd tell him where to—the same place she'd been thinking about all day.

Georgia took his hand in hers and tugged him up the street. "It's my turn to show you something," she said. Being a wedding planner did have its perks, one of them being that she was on good terms and knew the layout of some of the best hotels.

The Peabody would do nicely, Georgia decided. Clean, classy. Just the place for a little secret, dirty sex. She herded Linc through the lobby away from the marble fountain where the famous ducks played and depressed the call button for the elevator. Brunch would be over right now, meaning that the Skyway area would be virtually deserted.

The moment the elevator doors slid closed, she was on him. She wrapped her arms around his neck and tugged him closer, tasting him, feeding at his mouth. There was an insistent urgency about it, a desperateness she knew could only be caused by the fact that their time was drawing to a close. When they found Carter—and she didn't doubt that they would—her reason for being with Linc twenty-four-seven would be over. The thought almost made her whimper. He'd go back to his artistic badass bounty-hunter world and she'd return to making happily-ever-afters for everyone but herself.

Things would go back to normal…and yet she knew her normal would never be the same.

Linc cupped her rear end and growled low in his throat. "I love your ass."

Georgia slipped her hands down over his and squeezed, as well. "Yours is pretty damned nice, too."

The elevator glided to a stop, then the doors opened revealing a blessedly empty hallway. She grabbed his hand once more and propelled him toward the nearest bathroom. She tried to tug him into the ladies' room, but he balked.

"The mens' room gets less traffic and guys aren't

inclined to linger and fluff their hair and smear stuff on their faces. Come on," he said.

Though he was right, Georgia couldn't resist the impulse to argue. "I thought you were going to follow my lead," she growled.

The door had no sooner closed behind her when Linc pulled her into the handicapped stall and backed her against the door. "Your lead was misguided."

Then he kissed her deeply and she forgot to care.

Sensation and desire and the pure unadulterated need to simply have him inside her took over. Her hands went to the snap at his jeans while he tugged her sweater up and freed her breasts. He bent down and tugged a pouty nipple into his mouth, sighing against her as though he was a starving man and she was an all-you-can-eat buffet. Georgia made quick work of his pants and wrapped her hand around the length of him, feeling a heavy ache land in her womb as she touched him.

She was achy and hollow and needy, and the idea of Linc filling her up made her panties drench and her sex throb. She worked the slippery skin back and forth, felt him groan against her, his big calloused hands slide over the small of her back. He made her feel small and feminine, made her want unspeakable things. The air around them seemed to shimmer and vibrate with the glow of sexual heat.

"If you don't stop that we're going to be finished before we get started," he warned.

"Then how about moving your ass?" Georgia told him. "FYI—I'm ready." God, was she ready. She needed him now, didn't want to wait. Couldn't wait. She was frantic for him, desperate for him. She needed him now, not later. Hell, who was she kidding? She'd been needing him forever. She just hadn't known it.

Linc chuckled against her as she kicked her shoes off and out of the way. He put the condom on while she shucked her pants and, as he lifted her against the door and plunged into her, a huge sigh leaked out of her lungs.

Ah, there, she thought, inordinately relieved, her head dropping onto his shoulder.

She went boneless with relief, felt it all the way down to her curled toes. Need surpassed reason, longing trumped logic. She shouldn't want him, but she did. He was a fever in her blood, a parasite in her foolish heart, the very counterpart to her soul.

He was the disease and the cure, Georgia decided, and an antidote didn't exist to heal what ailed her.

And God help her when she couldn't get her fix.

LINC PUSHED INTO HER, covered her mouth with his own and savored her sigh of relief against his tongue.

Madness, the thought. Sheer madness. All day long he'd been doing his best to show her a good time without dragging her into the nearest bathroom. He'd wanted her all day, of course. He couldn't look at her without wanting her. *Needing* her, which was inherently much more frightening.

And yet, here they were—him following *her* lead, of all things—in a bathroom in one of the South's premiere hotels, getting it on like a couple of teenagers away from home on spring break.

She pulled his tongue into her mouth, inadvertently reminding him of the blow job she'd given him last night—*that sweet mouth closing over his dick, sucking him up like a Popsicle on the Fourth of July. Firelight dancing off of her wet curls. A warm blanket at his back and a hot female all over him.*

He almost came again just thinking about it.

And he was dangerously close anyway.

He pushed into her again, frantic to find release. Taking it slow wasn't an option, and since they were in a damned bathroom and she'd already told him she was ready, he didn't think he had to stand on ceremony and be a love machine. He wanted her and he was going to take her hard and fast, the way he'd been fantasizing about all friggin' day.

Linc powered into her, pumping wildly. In and out, in and out, harder and harder. She made little mewling sounds of pleasure, grunted and thrashed against him, riding his dick until he feared his legs would give way or his balls would break.

It was a testament to his insanity that he wouldn't care.

So long as she wanted him and he was inside of her, nothing mattered. The world existed to this particular moment in time—just him and her—and everything else faded into insignificance. A terrifying truth lay hidden in that thought, but Linc was too consumed with the orgasm gathering force in the back of his loins to care.

Georgia was almost there, as well. She sank her teeth into his shoulder, then licked the spot she'd hurt. He could feel her clamping around him, holding on to him with every bit of power she possessed. Unable to control himself, he pounded into her greedy body, pushed and pushed until he was certain someone was going to hear them, but he didn't give a damn. The only thing that mattered was her. Wanting him. Crying out his name.

"Oh, Linc," she whimpered brokenly. "I'm coming apart inside. You…make…me…crazy."

He pistoned in and out of her, pumped hard and fierce and angled high. "Welcome to my world, Trouble," he sighed. "Welcome to my world."

Georgia pumped and flexed harder against him.

She whimpered. She mewled. She swore. Her body suddenly went rigid and she clamped around him over and over again, triggering his own orgasm.

It rocketed from his loins with enough power to make his legs quake and his vision sparkle with white light, but at the moment he didn't give a damn. He didn't need to see, he only needed to feel. He locked his knees to keep them from giving way and held her to him while the last violent contractions of her own release milked his.

Breathing hard, shaken, Linc kissed her cheek and settled his forehead against hers. Smiling, she looked up at him and pressed a kiss to his jaw, the gesture sweet and endearing and should have been out of place after the wild, back-breaking sex they'd just shared.

Curiously, it wasn't.

He sighed contentedly and breathed in her delicious strawberry scent. "FYI," he said, throwing the line right back at her. "That was pretty damned wonderful."

Georgia chuckled and hugged him close. "FYI...I think you're pretty damned wonderful." She said it almost shyly, which was so out of character that Linc drew back to look at her.

And that's when he realized it—she wasn't talking about the sex.

She was talking about *him*.

His gaze tangled with hers and the genuine affection he saw mirrored back at him simultaneously filled his chest with warmth and dread.

Thankfully, his cell phone rang, preventing him from thinking about it, and in the time it took for him to find his phone and answer it, whatever he thought he might have seen in her pretty melting chocolate eyes was gone. Curiously, he didn't know whether to be happy or relieved.

In the end, it didn't matter.

"This was the call we've been waiting for," Linc told her, snapping the cell shut. "That was Lena at the Vacation Inn. Carter just checked in."

13

GEORGIA'S HEART SKIPPED a beat. "He's there? Now?"

"That's right," Linc said. He helped her with her sweater, then quickly righted himself, as well. "We're fifteen minutes out, twenty if traffic is bad, but if he's just now checking in then chances are he isn't going anywhere anytime soon."

Hurriedly struggling into her shoes, she hopped on one foot and snatched her purse from the floor. Linc was more than likely right about Carter not leaving in the time it took them to get there—he'd been right about everything else up to this point, after all—but Georgia didn't want to take any chances. The sooner they got to him, the better she'd feel. She didn't want the slimy bastard getting away from her and she wanted her mother's ring back.

Finally, she thought, as they hurried out of the bathroom, an amused bellhop in their wake. One way or another, she'd have some answers. Naturally, she hoped Carter had the ring in his possession, that he hadn't had time to sell it. Unfortunately, if he'd checked into a hotel and wasn't sleeping in his car, then it was all too possible that he'd managed to finally unload her ring.

The idea sent a shot of fear into her veins, but she knew she had to be realistic. She didn't want to, but Linc had left her no choice. He'd repeatedly told her that just because they found Carter didn't mean they'd find her ring. She knew that, but she just couldn't seem to make herself accept it. In the event that he didn't have it, then she'd simply have to start her search over, but she'd never give up.

Her gaze slid to Linc as he stepped into the waiting elevator. Either way, she'd be giving him up, she thought woodenly. A pang of regret so intense it brought tears to her eyes kicked her in the stomach, but she blinked them away and told herself she was merely emotional. This miserable ache in her chest couldn't possibly mean what she suspected it did.

It was too soon. He couldn't be the right guy for her. She hadn't *known* the instant she'd seen him the way her parents had. She hadn't been bowled over with emotion. She hadn't heard bells or seen stars— other than the ones bursting behind her lids when he'd made love to her—or any of the other stories she'd heard in her line of work.

Georgia straightened. Nah, she thought, pulling in a bracing breath. Couldn't be. She wouldn't let it. In just a little while she would have to dump her pretend boyfriend and that would be that. If she thought about the fact that they'd just made love for the last time, she'd fall apart, and doing this right with Carter—getting her mother's ring back—had to take first priority. It was actually a relief to be able to focus on something else. She'd have time enough to fall apart later.

"I'm going to call Cade and let him know what's going on," Linc said. He reached for his cell phone.

"Oh, you're not going to need any backup," Georgia told him, rocking back in her heels, a determined growl in her voice.

He grinned at her, that endearingly wicked smile reaching his eyes. "I hate to break it to you, Trouble, but I wouldn't need it if you *weren't* with me."

Georgia felt her lips twitch and resisted the urge to roll her eyes. "I know that. I'm not trying to impugn your masculinity or imply that you can't take care of Carter yourself," she said, waving an airy hand. "It's just…*I want to.*" She paused, her jaw clenched so tight she thought she felt a tooth crack. "You know, I've never been a violent person, but I want to *hurt* him. I really do." She looked up at him and frowned. "Does that make me a terrible person?"

"No, Georgia. It makes you human. He's hurt you. He's taken something important away from you. Revenge is a perfectly normal emotion." He pulled a shrug as the elevator landed on the ground floor. "Or it's normal in my world, anyway."

Georgia nodded, silently thanking him for giving her the validation she'd needed. She wasn't accustomed to doubting herself, but this was all new territory for her.

They hurriedly made their way to the parking lot where they'd left the SUV and soon they were on their way. Thanks to some excellent defensive driving on Linc's part, eleven minutes later—she knew because she'd looked at the clock—they were sitting in front of the Vacation Inn.

The hotel was one of those circa nineteen-seventies designs—a two-story brick with room doors facing the parking lot, convenient for the speedy, thrifty traveler who didn't want to haul luggage through a lobby. This, Linc had pointed out, worked to their advantage.

Afraid of losing her job, Lena's help had only gone so far as to say that Carter had checked into the hotel and was in a ground-floor unit.

"There's his car," Georgia said, recognizing the make and model. Determination and anger and hope all congealed in her belly. She withdrew her stun gun from her purse and slipped it into her pocket where it landed with a reassuring weight.

Linc grinned at her and shook his head. "Feel better now that you're packing?"

"I'm not going to feel good until I hit him with it."

He arched a single brow and winced. "You know that if he doesn't resist, technically I'm not supposed to hurt anybody."

"Then I guess it's a good thing you won't be the one jolting him, isn't it?"

Linc merely chuckled and parked a few doors down. He surveyed the scene, then pointed to the door just to the left of where Carter's car sat. "He's in that one."

Georgia peered at where he'd indicated. "How do you know?"

"Because the curtains are drawn. The two on either side of him are open, meaning that they're vacant."

She smiled, impressed. And that's why he was the bounty hunter, Georgia thought. "Okay, let's—"

"Uh-uh," Linc told her. "There's no *let's* on this to start with. I'm going to get him, you can talk to him once I've got him."

"Linc!"

"I mean it, Georgia. He could be dangerous. I'm not letting you go to the door."

"He's a petty thief, not a murderer!" she said, her

voice bordering on a scream. She couldn't believe he was doing this. He knew how important this was to her, dammit.

"And you're a wedding planner with a stun gun in your pocket. People do strange things when they're angry or cornered." He pinned her with a glare. "I told you from the get-go that you'd have to follow my rules to the letter, follow my lead and that I was in charge. You agreed, right?"

"Yes, but—"

"But nothing. I'll bring him out. Then you can take your shot at him. That's how we're going to do this. Understood?"

Though she knew he was right, she still didn't like being told to wait in the car like a kid who wasn't allowed to go into the grocery store. She lifted her chin and glared mutinously at him. "Understood," she all but choked out.

"Good." He consulted the picture of Carter he had once more, then morphed into bounty-hunter mode right before her eyes. He slipped into a multi-pocketed vest which was outfitted with everything he might need—flashlight, mace, handcuffs, gun.

For whatever reason, the sight of the gun jolted her to her senses. He could get hurt, Georgia realized, suddenly feeling small and petty for arguing with him when he'd only been trying to protect her.

He turned to go and she stayed him with a hand on the arm. "I'm sorry," she said. "Be careful."

Something moved behind his gaze, then he leaned over and pressed a kiss to her lips. "Always," he said.

Georgia released an uneasy breath as she watched Linc walk up the sidewalk and rap on Carter's door. "Pizza delivery," she heard him call.

Less than half a minute later, the thieving SOB opened the door. "I didn't order—"

"Carter Watkins?" Linc asked.

Carter scowled. "Who wants to—"

Without warning Linc slammed his fist into Carter's jaw, sending him flying backward into the room. Georgia gasped, then squealed and pressed a hand against her mouth. He'd thrown that punch for her, she knew. It was a blatant act of masculinity on her behalf, and her giddy, bloodthirsty little heart absolutely soared as a result of it.

Linc dragged him outside, pinned him against the wall and handcuffed him, then motioned for Georgia to come and join him. Adrenaline and nerves making her shake like a leaf in a windstorm, she hurried to Linc's side and looked up at Carter. His lip was busted and blood spurted from his nose.

The fool actually smiled when he saw her. "Georgia?"

"Where's the ring, Carter?" she demanded, her voice cracking with every bit of anger she'd been holding on to since she'd realized he'd stolen it from her.

He paled. "Ring?"

Linc shook him hard enough to rattle his teeth. "Don't play dumb. Answer the woman's questions and I won't kick your ass all the way to two-oh-one Poplar."

Evidently recognizing the address to the jail, Carter's wild-eyed gaze darted between them. "I don't have it anymore," he said. "I sold it."

Her heart sagged and she tried not to panic. It was a futile effort. Her throat clogged and she swore.

"To who?" Linc asked, clearly sensing that she was on the verge of a breakdown.

"I—I don't know," Carter said. "Just some guy."

"Did you pawn it, you miserable bastard?" Georgia asked. "Did you pawn my mother's ring?"

Carter's eyes widened and he gave his head a small shake. "No, I d-didn't pawn it. I tried," he said. "But I couldn't get anything for it. The guy said it was worthless."

Worthless.

A year and half of her father's time and effort, a testament to determination and unwavering faith, the eternal symbol of her parents' love, a precious heirloom she'd wanted to pass along to her children...*worthless.*

Gone, possibly forever, because of her. Her gaze narrowed on Carter.

Because of him.

A red haze of anger swam before her eyes, and before she realized what she was doing, she drew back and sucker punched him right in his soft gut.

He grunted and doubled over in pain. "She hit me," Carter wheezed, thunderstruck.

Linc snorted. "Consider yourself lucky," he told Carter. "She'd planned on hitting you with her—"

Georgia withdrew the stun gun from her pocket and coolly zapped him on the chest. His eyes widened, then glazed over and spit dribbled from his mouth before he crumpled to the ground in a twitching heap at their feet.

"—stun gun," Linc finished, his gaze bouncing between the two of them.

Drained, miserable and momentarily hopeless, Georgia stared at Linc. She pulled a small shrug. "It'll be easier for you to get him in the car this way."

And that, she knew, was going to be the easiest thing they would do over the next hour, but at least it would give her time to prepare for the hardest. She swallowed tightly and put her game face on.

Namely saying goodbye to Linc.

"I'M SORRY, GEORGIA," Linc told her, feeling as helpless as he'd ever been in his adult life. This was exactly what he'd feared, what he'd tried to prepare her for. "I was hoping I'd find it in his stuff, but he only had a couple of changes of clothes, some cheap cologne and twenty-seven bucks in his wallet." Loser, Linc thought, disgusted. No doubt the twenty-seven bucks was what was left over from the sale of her mother's ring after he'd paid for his hotel room.

Though Georgia hadn't shed a tear, Linc knew she was coming apart on the inside. It was as though she'd turned herself off, put everything in lockdown mode. She currently sat in the passenger seat of his truck, her hands folded primly in her lap, her face an emotionless mask that was distinctly unnerving.

"Do you want me to take you to get something to eat?" he offered. It was lame, he knew, but he couldn't think of anything else to say. They'd already returned Carter to the police station, and he'd picked up his body receipt to give to Marlene. Technically, he'd fulfilled his part of the bargain and yet the idea of leaving her…

Christ, he just couldn't. No, there was more.

He didn't want to.

And he wouldn't, Linc decided, knowing that he'd just gone from dangerous waters to completely in over his head. Oh, hell. Who was he kidding?

He'd been in over his head from the beginning. Had known that she'd be the end of him.

But he simply couldn't leave her like this. He wanted to hold her and rock her and make it all better. Soothe the hurt, be her rock, her secret hiding place, her knight in shining armor. Her…everything, he realized.

Mostly, he wanted to throttle the hell out of Carter Watkins for hurting her in the first place.

A wan smile tugged at his lips. Of course, Georgia had done a pretty good job of roughing him up herself. He'd been alternately stunned and proud when she'd thrown that punch at him a little while ago. He'd known she'd planned to use the stun gun, but had never anticipated that she'd deck him, too. For such a little person, she'd put a surprising amount of force behind the blow.

"Thanks," she said wearily. "But I'm not hungry. I'd really like to just go home."

Linc nodded. "Sure."

They drove in silence, her seemingly lost in her own thoughts, him unreasonably nervous, miserable and frustrated because he was so powerless to make things right. He reached over and grabbed her hand, then gave it a gentle squeeze. She looked at him then and the anguish in those tortured brown eyes— the pain she was hiding from him—slammed into him, making him feel even more helpless. A finger of unease nudged his belly, a premonition of dread he didn't quite understand, but recognized all the same. Every sense went on point.

Linc pulled up behind her car and shifted into Park. He turned to get out of the SUV and felt her hand land upon his arm.

"You don't have to stay."

He frowned, the sinking pit in his stomach becoming a yawning hole that threatened to consume him. "I—"

She squeezed her eyes tightly shut. "Linc, it's okay. You— You don't have to stay." She gave a little unnatural laugh. "Consider yourself dumped. I'll, uh— I'll inform my brother, per our agreement." She chuckled again, as though doing so would make this funny. "You did what you said you would do for me—you found Carter—and for that I thank you. I'll be getting in touch with Gracie soon so that we can start planning her wedding."

"Georgia," Linc sighed, her name more of a plea than anything else. His gaze searched hers, looking for any sort of foothold and finding none. "We'll keep looking for the ring. I'll help you. I'll talk to Carter and see—"

"Thanks, but no," she said, her voice pleasant but firm. No doubt that was the tone she used with her mothers-of-the-brides and moody grooms who didn't want to be fitted for their tuxes, Linc decided as something in his chest rattled around and broke. "I can handle it from here."

A bark of dry laughter erupted from his throat and he stared at her for a minute, wondering if she'd change her mind, if this was a joke, or a bad dream. Surely she wasn't doing this to him. Surely she wasn't kicking him to the curb simply because he could no longer be of service to her. Surely the past few days had meant more to her than that?

Apparently not, Linc decided as Georgia gathered her purse, opened the door and slid out of his truck.

Out of his life.

She paused, offered a tentative smile, but didn't meet his gaze. "I'll, uh— I guess I'll see you around."

"So I'm disposable now, eh?" he asked, the irony not lost on him at all.

A sad smile shaped her lips and those dark, dark eyes finally found his. "You can't complain, Linc. I'm just following your lead."

And with that parting comment, she turned and walked away.

14

THOUGH IT TOOK every ounce of strength she possessed. Georgia made it into her back door before she fell apart. She dropped her purse onto the counter, pushed her hands into her hair, then slid down the wall and let the sob she'd been holding back for the past hour and a half rip out of her.

Between the ring being gone—probably forever, though she'd keep looking—and "dumping" Linc, she felt like her insides had been put through a stump grinder, then dumped into a gristmill.

In short, *shattered*.

The instant the call came in about Carter, she'd known she was going to have to face this, but somehow knowing it and being prepared were two completely different things. She'd used the looming rendezvous with Carter to suspend thinking about the inevitable "break up" with Linc, but the minute Carter had told her that he no longer had the ring, saying goodbye to Linc had taken prominence.

She'd known, hadn't she, that this would be the inevitable outcome? She'd known from the minute she'd laid eyes on him that he wasn't the type to settle down, that he saw love as a weakness, not a blessing to be nurtured and cherished.

That's why she'd insisted that she break up with him. That's why every time he did something that made her silly heart melt, she'd reminded herself that he thought fools fell in love and only complete idiots got married. Hell, he was so commitment-phobic he wouldn't even go back to her store.

That, in and of itself, was enough to set off every warning bell in the known universe. Or at the very least, hers.

She'd known…and yet that hadn't stopped her from falling head over heels in love with him.

But what good was love if it wasn't returned? If you never got it back? Georgia wanted her own wedding, her own happily ever after. Her own children running around and tugging on her pants' leg. She wanted an affectionate hug, a partner for her tub, someone to share the dawns with her. She wanted a guy who wanted more than *just her,* but to *share* her life with her. She wiped the tears from her eyes with the edge of her shirt, drew her knees up to her chest and leaned her head against the wall. Another whimper shook her chest. Bogey and Bacall rubbed against her legs and Stitch licked her hand, making another sob rattle loose.

She wanted what her parents had. She knew it was out there somewhere. She knew she deserved it and more importantly, she knew she wasn't willing to settle for anything less.

Considering all that—point A to point B in the most efficient fashion—she also knew cutting Linc loose was the most practical thing for her to do. He'd never commit and she'd never settle, and that put them at opposing goals.

She managed a watery smile, closed her eyes and let the tears fall.

And *that* was the height of inefficiency.

"YOU'RE AN IDIOT."

Gritty-eyed and unshaven, Linc looked up from the newspaper he'd been reading and stared at is brother. "Piss off, Cade. I'm not in the mood."

"I don't give a damn whether you're in the mood or not. You can't keep on like this. Just go find the damned ring already and quit trying to pick up skips, too. Martin and I can handle it."

Thanks to Georgia's team-up-with-a-politician idea, their previously lagging business had suddenly boomed. In fact, though it had always been a family-run business, taking on another bounty hunter to help with the slack was becoming a very real possibility.

He passed a hand over his face. "I'm fine."

"You're not fine."

"Leave it," Linc growled.

"Do you want me to go have a chat with Carter? Scare a little more information out of him?"

Linc sighed. That was Cade, always looking out for him. Always at his back.

Unfortunately, there was nothing his brother could do for him this time.

This time he had to straighten out his own mess and fight his own fight.

"I threatened to tell everybody in his cell that he was a cross-dressing pedophile," Linc said flatly. "He's been in jail enough to know what happens to men who hurt kids. Believe me, I've scared everything out of him that can be scared. The bastard has told me everything he knows." He sighed, massaged the bridge of his nose. "All I can do is keep looking. Keep canvasing. At some point, I'll find who he sold it to." The bastard had duped a suit on Union Avenue. Unfortunately he didn't remember exactly where, but after a little persuading on Linc's part, had managed to narrow it down to a several-block stretch.

Cade frowned. "Does Georgia know you're doing

this? That you've been at this for two weeks nonstop?"

"No, she doesn't, and I don't want her to. I've told Gracie to keep her mouth shut and I expect you to do the same. When I find it, I'll tell her myself."

"Little brother, I know this is none of my business, but I hate to see you get hurt." He hesitated. "Are you sure she's worth this?"

Linc felt a tired smile roll around his lips. "Cade, I have never been more certain of anything in my life. She's a lot of trouble, but she's my Trouble." Immediately a vision of sweet brown eyes, lush lips and a heart-shaped rear end invaded his thoughts, sending a pang of regret into his chest and a dart of heat into his loins. He paused, then looked up at his brother and uttered a helpless laugh. "You're not going to believe this, but I'm—" He shook his head, still not quite able to make it process. "I'm in love with her."

Cade's eyes widened and he guffawed. "I'm not going to believe it? *I'm* not going to believe it," he repeated. "You moron, the only two people who haven't realized you're in love with her are you and Georgia Hart. The rest of us knew the minute you suspended the rest of your caseload and spent every waking minute with her." He laughed again. "Why don't you just go tell her how you feel? Why are you putting yourself through all of this?"

Linc shared the story behind the ring. "A year and a half, Cade. *A year and a half.* I've only been looking for the damned thing for two weeks."

Cade inclined his head. "Martin would have done that for Mom, you know. He loved her that much."

Linc snorted. "And it almost destroyed him. I swore I'd never let myself do that, that I'd never be so dependent on someone else for my own happiness and yet here I am, canvassing Union freakin' Avenue—one of the longest damned streets in the city—for a worthless ring with priceless sentimental value."

"Because you love her."

He nodded, letting the weight of the sentiment wash over him. He swallowed tightly. "Because I love her."

"What are you going to do when you find it?"

Linc grinned. "What the hell do you think, fool? I'm going to propose."

Two and half months later…

Her mouth dry, her heart racing, Georgia stood next to Karen at the counter near the bathroom sink in her store and stared at the little white stick which had the potential to completely change Georgia's life forever.

Babies tended to do that.

Karen gasped and her gaze flew to Georgia's. "It's positive," she breathed, her face wreathed in a joyous smile, dimples winking in both cheeks.

"It's positive," Georgia repeated faintly. She dropped onto the toilet seat and stared at the wall.

Beaming, Karen bounced up and down on the balls of her feet. "It's *positive!*" she squealed. "You're pregnant! Ohmigod, ohmigod, ohmigod! I'm going to be an honorary aunt—maybe a real one if your brother comes around," she added.

She and Linc might have called it quits, but surprisingly Jack and Karen had been seeing each other ever since Jack had asked Karen to spy for him. Funny how things had worked out, Georgia thought, happy for her friend.

"We're going to have a baby," Karen breathed, still talking more to herself than Georgia. "We're going to decorate a nursery and buy little bootees." She sighed, her eyes watering. "Oh, Georgia. I'm so happy for you." She paused. "Are you okay? You look a little pale."

"We used protection," she said dimly, still trying to absorb the fact that she was pregnant. With Linc Stone's baby. "I'm not supposed to be pregnant."

"Protection isn't foolproof, as evidenced by the fact that you are going to have a baby," Karen said happily, gesturing toward the test. She suddenly frowned. "You've always said you wanted kids. You're happy, right?"

She was more than happy, she was ecstatic. She was just a little shell-shocked. She'd assumed that she'd missed the last couple of periods because she'd been an emotional wreck—being pregnant had never occurred to her. Then this morning her biscuit and jam had made an encore appearance and she'd noticed a tenderness in her breasts that hadn't ever been there before. She'd bought the test more as a whim than anything else and yet...she was pregnant.

Immediately an image of a little boy with espresso curls and mossy green eyes leaped into her mind and a slow, tremulous smile slid over her lips. Tears welled in her eyes.

"Karen," she said wonderingly. "I'm going to have a baby." She heard the bell ring, signaling a customer had entered the store, but she didn't have the presence of mind to deal with someone else's joy at the moment. She wanted to savor her own. She'd learned that from Linc, if nothing else.

A baby.

His baby.

"What are you going to do about Linc?" Karen asked as though reading her mind.

There was no question about that. "I'll have to tell him."

Frankly, she didn't know how he'd react. She was assuming that since he never wanted to marry he never wanted kids, but wanted or not, she was having this baby. She would tell him, of course, because it was the right thing to do, but she wouldn't expect anything out of him and certainly wouldn't make any demands. She was fully capable of supporting a child on her own and, as far as a male influence went, she had Jack. It might not be the ideal situation, but it was the one she had. She would make it work.

Besides, considering that Linc Stone would forever own her heart, she knew she had a precious little shot of ever getting it back to give to someone else. She rubbed her hand over her belly where their baby currently grew and felt tears burn the backs of her lids and a lump the size of a plum well in her throat.

She wouldn't have Linc—hadn't heard from him since he'd pulled out of driveway more than two months ago—but at least she'd have a little part of him.

"A customer came in," Georgia said. "Do you think you could go check on them? I want a few minutes to myself to sort of let this sink in."

Karen hugged her tight. "Sure."

Okay, Georgia thought, immediately going into

list-making mode. First things first. She'd have to make an appointment with an OB. She needed to get on some vitamin supplements. Then there was life insur—

"Georgia, could you come out here a minute, please?" Karen called, her voice curiously strangled.

Dammit, she'd just asked for a few minutes. Karen had been so good about handling things over the past couple of months. Georgia stood and wiped a little mascara from beneath her eye. She'd picked a damned annoying time to revert to her old habits.

"It's *important*," Karen called again, as though reading her mind. "Otherwise I wouldn't bother you."

It had better be important, Georgia thought, striding into the showroom. Her gaze landed on Linc and she drew up short. Emotion broadsided her and her body went into numb shakes on the inside, rattling her to the core. Those long locks definitely hadn't seen a pair of scissors since she'd last seen him, and there was a weariness around those beautiful, woefully familiar eyes that tugged at her heartstrings. What was he doing here? she wondered. Why now, of all times?

Karen's gaze darted between the two of them and she wore a smile that bordered on euphoric.

"Hey, Trouble," he said, his gaze drifting all over her, seemingly drinking her in. He looked tired, but happy, strained and just a little bit…scared.

"What are you doing here?" she breathed, stunned, giving voice to the question. Her heart jumped into her already crowded throat and her pulse triple-timed it in her veins. What little moisture she had in her mouth instantly vanished.

"I brought you a present."

She frowned. "A present?"

Ducking to avoid the tulle hanging from the ceiling Linc made his way toward her. "It's taken three months, hardly the year and half that your father looked for it, but—" he withdrew her mother's ring from his pocket, making her breath catch and a startled gasp slip from her mouth "—I finally found it."

Her vision blurred with tears, Georgia carefully took the ring from his fingers and inspected the stone. Just as flawed as she remembered, but perfect all the same. Her gaze flew to Linc's. "How did you do this? Where did you find it?"

Linc shoved his hands into his pockets. "Carter sold it to a guy on Union Avenue. Operating on the assumption that he was a local who was in the area for business—and that he'd be back every day—I kept going back and asking questions. I finally found him and made him an offer he couldn't refuse."

Sweet God in heaven, she thought, her heart bursting with joy. He'd gone back and looked for it. She had, too, but had clearly been going to the wrong area. And he was here, with the ring, in her shop. A place she never imagined to see him again.

Her shimmering gaze tangled with his. "I—I can't believe you did this for me."

He shifted, looked away, then those mossy green eyes caught hers once more. "Funny what a guy'll do for love, eh?"

Karen squealed from her post behind the counter.

"A guy'll do for love?" Was he saying what she thought he was saying?

"Yeah. If you'd give that ring back for a second, I've got plans for it."

Intrigued, Georgia cocked her head, but handed it over all the same. He'd given it to her once, after all. She knew she could trust him to give it back.

Smiling, Linc went down on bended knee, looked up at her and cleared his throat. "Georgia Hart, I love you. Would you do me the honor of becoming my wife?" He jerked his head toward the front window and his lips slid into that woefully familiar, wicked endearing grin. "And would you please wear that dress to our wedding because I've been imagining you in it since the first moment I stepped foot in this store."

Confused, she felt a line emerge between her brows. He'd been imagining her in it since— Her racing heart did a little figure eight in her chest and a smile bloomed across her lips. "*That's* why you wouldn't come back here?" she asked. "*That's* why you avoided the store?"

Linc ducked his head. "I'm not proud," he admitted. "But I've seen the error of my ways."

"B-but I haven't heard from you. You haven't so much as called me."

"That's because I was looking for the ring, planning this special moment," he said, his teeth partially gritted. "And you're arguing. Have you noticed that I am actually on my knee? Do you see that? I've made a proper proposal and you haven't had the decency to answer me yet?"

"Yes, I see it. I'm just trying to decide if I want to be pissed off at you or not."

"How about deciding if you want to marry me or not, Trouble," he said, exasperated. "After all, that's why I'm here."

"Well, of course I want to marry you. But I can still be pissed off."

A grin easing over his face, Linc stood and wrapped his arms around her, then kissed her until her knees wobbled. Hot, wild, thrilling and familiar. *Hers.* He carefully slipped the ring on to her finger. "I don't doubt that one bit."

She chuckled against his mouth. "Careful, dickwad, we don't want to start out our engagement in a fight."

Linc heaved a long-suffering sigh. "What have I told you about that nickname?"

"That you don't like it."

"Right. Do you think you could come up with something a little more flattering?"

Smiling, Georgia drew back and looked up at him. Excitement and joy tangled inside her. "How about Daddy?"

He blinked. "Daddy? But—" His eyes widened. "You're—"

"She is!" Karen exclaimed, evidently unable to control herself.

Another grin slid over his lips and he dropped his forehead against hers. "We've got to do something about her."

"Forget about her," Georgia said, her body going into a slow simmer. "Let's do something about us."

Linc grinned again, then bent his head and brushed a promising kiss over her lips. "Just follow my lead, sweetheart. Just follow my lead."

* * * * *

*One Stone brother has been brought down,
but there's another still at large.
Don't miss the fireworks when
Cade meets his match in
THE BIG HEAT by Jennifer LaBrecque,
available next month.*

Brad shoved the truck into gear and drove to the bottom of the hill, where the road forked. Turn left, and he'd be home in five minutes. Turn right, and he was headed for Indian Rock.

He had no damn business going to Indian Rock.

He had nothing to say to Meg McKettrick, and if he never set eyes on the woman again, it would be two weeks too soon.

He turned right.

He couldn't have said why.

He just drove straight to the Dixie Dog Drive-In.

Back in the day, he and Meg used to meet at the Dixie Dog, by tacit agreement, when either of them had been away. It had been some kind of universe thing, purely intuitive.

Passing familiar landmarks, Brad told himself he ought to turn around. The old days were gone. Things had ended badly between him and Meg anyhow, and she wasn't going to be at the Dixie Dog.

He kept driving.

He rounded a bend, and there was the Dixie Dog. Its big neon sign, a giant hot dog, was all lit up and going through its corny sequence—first it was covered in red squiggles of light, meant to suggest ketchup, and then yellow, for mustard.

Brad pulled into one of the slots next to a speaker, rolled down the truck window and ordered.

A girl roller-skated out with the order about five minutes later.

When she wheeled up to the driver's window, smiling, her eyes went wide with recognition, and she dropped the tray with a clatter.

Silently Brad swore. Damn if he hadn't forgotten he was a famous country singer.

The girl, a skinny thing wearing too much eye makeup, immediately started to cry. "I'm sorry!" she sobbed, squatting to gather up the mess.

"It's okay," Brad answered quietly, leaning to look down at her, catching a glimpse of her plastic name tag. "It's okay, Mandy. No harm done."

"I'll get you another dog and a shake right away, Mr. O'Ballivan!"

"Mandy?"

She stared up at him pitifully, sniffling. Thanks to the copious tears, most of the goop on her eyes had slid south. "Yes?"

"When you go back inside, could you not mention seeing me?"

"But you're Brad O'Ballivan!"

"Yeah," he answered, suppressing a sigh. "I know."

She rolled a little closer. "You wouldn't happen to have a picture you could autograph for me, would you?"

"Not with me," Brad answered.

"You could sign this napkin, though," Mandy said. "It's only got a little chocolate on the corner."

Brad took the paper napkin and her order pen, and scrawled his name. Handed both items back through the window.

She turned and whizzed back toward the side entrance to the Dixie Dog.

Brad waited, marveling that he hadn't considered incidents like this one before he'd decided to come back home. In retrospect, it seemed shortsighted, to say the least, but the truth was, he'd expected to be—Brad O'Ballivan.

Presently Mandy skated back out again, and this time she managed to hold on to the tray.

"I didn't tell a soul!" she whispered. "But Heather and Darlene *both* asked me why my mascara was all smeared." Efficiently she hooked the tray onto the bottom edge of the window.

Brad extended payment, but Mandy shook her head.

"The boss said it's on the house, since I dumped your first order on the ground."

He smiled. "Okay, then. Thanks."

Mandy retreated, and Brad was just reaching for the food when a bright red Blazer whipped into the space beside his. The driver's door sprang open, crashing into the metal speaker, and somebody got out in a hurry.

Something quickened inside Brad.

And in the next moment Meg McKettrick was standing practically on his running board, her blue eyes blazing.

Brad grinned. "I guess you're not over me after all," he said.

REQUEST YOUR FREE BOOKS!

2 FREE NOVELS PLUS 2 FREE GIFTS!

HARLEQUIN®

Blaze

Red-hot reads!

HB07

Get ready to meet

THREE WISE WOMEN

with stories by

DONNA BIRDSELL, LISA CHILDS

and

SUSAN CROSBY.

Don't miss these three unforgettable stories about modern-day women and the love and new lives they find on Christmas.

Look for *Three Wise Women*
Available December wherever you buy books.

THE ITALIAN BILLIONAIRE'S CHRISTMAS MIRACLE
by *Catherine Spencer*
Book #: 2688

Domenico Silvaggio d'Avalos knows that beautiful,
unworldly Arlene Russell isn't mistress material—
but might she be suitable as his wife?

HIS CHRISTMAS BRIDE
by *Helen Brooks*
Book #: 2689

Powerful billionaire Zak Hamilton understood
Blossom's vulnerabilities, and he had to have her.
What was more, he'd make sure he claimed her
as his bride—by Christmas!

Be sure not to miss out on these two fabulous
Christmas stories available December 2007,
brought to you by Harlequin Presents!

HARLEQUIN® Presents®

RED HOT REVENGE

There are times in a man's life...
when only seduction will settle old scores!

This is

Jennie Lucas's

debut book—be sure not to miss out on
a brilliant story from a fabulous new author!

THE GREEK
BILLIONAIRE'S
BABY REVENGE

Book #2690

When Nikos installed a new mistress, Anna fled.
Now Nikos is furious when he discovers Anna's
taken his son. He vows to possess Anna, and make
her learn who's boss!

Look out for more from Jennie coming soon!

**Available in December 2007
only from Harlequin Presents.**

Pick up our exciting series of revenge-filled romances—
they're recommended and red-hot!

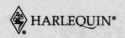

American ★ Romance®

Kate Merrill had grown up convinced
that the most attractive men were incapable
of ever settling down. Yet the harder she
resisted the superstar photographer
Tyler Nichols, the more persistent the
handsome world traveler became.
So by the time Christmas arrived, there
was only one wish on her holiday list—
that she was wrong!

LOOK FOR

THE CHRISTMAS DATE

BY

Michele Dunaway

Available December
wherever you buy books

HARLEQUIN®
Blaze™

COMING NEXT MONTH

#363 A BLAZING LITTLE CHRISTMAS Jacquie D'Alessandro, Joanne Rock, Kathleen O'Reilly
A sizzling Christmas anthology
When a freak snowstorm strands three couples at the Timberline Lodge for the holidays, anything is possible...including incredible sex! Cozy up to these sizzling Christmas stories that prove that a "blazing ever after" is the best gift of all....

#364 STROKES OF MIDNIGHT Hope Tarr
The Wrong Bed
When author Becky Stone's horoscope predicted that the New Year would bring her great things, she never expected the first thing she'd experience would be *a great one-night stand!* Or that her New Year's fling would last the whole year through....

#365 TALKING IN YOUR SLEEP... Samantha Hunter
It's almost Christmas and all Rafe Moore can hear...is sexy whispering right in his ear. Next-door neighbor Joy Clarke is talking in her sleep and it's keeping Rafe up at night. Rafe's ready to explore her whispered desires. Problem is, in the light of day, Joy doesn't recall a thing!

#366 BABY, IT'S COLD OUTSIDE Cathy Yardley
And that's why Colin Reeves and Emily Stanfield head indoors—then it's sparks, sensual heat and hot times ahead! But will their private holiday hometown reunion last longer than forty-eight delicious hours in bed?

#367 THE BIG HEAT Jennifer LaBrecque
Big, Bad Bounty Hunters, Bk. 2
When Cade Stone agreed to keep an eye on smart-mouthed Sunny Templeton, he figured it wouldn't be too hard. After all, all she'd done was try to take out a politician. Who wouldn't do the same thing? Cade knew she wasn't a threat to jump bail. Too bad he hadn't counted on her wanting to jump him....

#368 WHAT SHE *REALLY* WANTS FOR CHRISTMAS Debbi Rawlins
Million Dollar Secrets, Bk. 6
Liza Skinner, lottery winner wannabe, *thinks* she knows the kind of guy she should be with, but is she ever wrong! Dr. Evan Gann is just the one to show her that a buttoned-down type can have a wild side and still come through for her when she needs him most....

www.eHarlequin.com

HBCNM1107